THE ENTIRELY TRUE STORY OF THE UNBELIEVABLE FIB

ADAM SHAUGHNESSY

Algonquin Young Readers   2015

Published by
Algonquin Young Readers
an imprint of Algonquin Books of Chapel Hill
Post Office Box 2225
Chapel Hill, North Carolina 27515-2225

a division of
Workman Publishing
225 Varick Street
New York, New York 10014

LIBRARY OF CONGRESS CATALOGING-IN-PUBLICATION DATA
Shaughnessy, Adam, [date]
The entirely true story of the unbelievable FIB / by Adam Shaughnessy.—
First edition.
        pages cm
Summary: When eleven-year-old Pru and new kid ABE discover another
world beneath their quiet town, where Viking gods lurk just out of sight,
they must race to secure the Eye of Odin, source of all knowledge—and the
key to stopping a war that could destroy both human and immortal realms.
ISBN 978-1-61620-498-3
[1. Gods, Norse—Fiction. 2. Mythology, Norse—Fiction. 3. Magic—
Fiction. 4. Fantasy.] I. Title.
PZ7.1.S49En 2015
[Fic]—dc23   2015010989

10 9 8 7 6 5 4 3 2 1

First Edition

For my mother, who filled my childhood
with love and stories.

CHAPTER 1

THE ENVELOPES ARRIVED DURING THE UNCERTAIN hours of Thursday morning—those dark, early hours between tomorrow and yesterday, between not-quite-yet and nevermore. It's a time when the day is still young, still taking shape, and still open to possibility.

The envelopes did not arrive in mailboxes or through mail slots, nor did they arrive with any sort of postage or return address. Instead, unseen hands slipped the mysterious letters beneath bedroom doors throughout the small New England community of Middleton.

One might imagine that such a strange occurrence would create alarm and worry. Under normal circumstances, one would be right. In this case, however, the curious deliveries failed to raise concern because most people never saw the envelopes. People lead busy lives, after all, and the envelopes were easy to miss.

One could even say that the envelopes were hard to see.

In fact, of all the people in Middleton, only one girl who received an envelope truly saw it. Prudence Potts did more than see it, actually.

She opened it.

Inside waited what appeared to be a postcard. Its face might have been white at one time, but the passing of days had added wrinkles and spots, and shifted the hue to a yellowish-brown. A handwritten message remained visible, however.

It read:

Be grave in your search,
and avoid having stones in your head.

The back of the card bore more writing, golden letters across an inky field of deep midnight blue. Unfortunately, this additional text did nothing to explain the cryptic words on the card's face. In fact, the sentence written in gold was a question.

Prudence was eleven years old. She had a bob of red hair and a spattering of freckles that lay in reckless disarray across her nose. She considered herself a

2

detective, of sorts, just like her dad had been. As such, she had a particular interest in questions. Questions were like mysteries. Both demanded answers.

Pru was especially drawn to the question on the card. It asked:

WHAT IS THE UNBELIEVABLE FIB?

CHAPTER 2

SEVERAL HOURS AFTER DISCOVERING THE ENVELOPE in her room, Pru stood with her classmates in front of the great stone mansion known as Winterhaven House. A swirling mass of dark clouds blanketed the sky over Pru's head. They had settled over Middleton that very morning, as dark and heavy as a bad mood.

A storm was coming.

Still, Pru was willing to brave storms if it meant spending the day on a field trip and away from Mrs. Edleman's sixth-grade classroom. She just wished she could have left Mrs. Edleman behind as easily as the other antique fixtures of Middleton Elementary School. Her teacher was, at that moment, going over her Rules for Good Behavior one last time.

Pru hoped it was the last time, anyway.

She studied the clouds until her teacher paused for breath.

"Are there any questions?" Mrs. Edleman concluded with the stern sort of look that teachers use to suggest that there really ought not to be any questions at all.

Pru raised her hand.

Mrs. Edleman paused. She adjusted her glasses on the bridge of her nose. Pru glimpsed her teacher's lips moving slightly.

Pru had practiced a great many detective skills in her drive to follow in her dad's footsteps. And while some of her explorations had led to disappointment (she was a disaster when it came to lifting fingerprints, for example), other explorations had proved to be a surprising success. One such success had come when Pru discovered an uncanny talent for reading lips. From what she could see of Mrs. Edleman, she strongly suspected her teacher was counting silently to ten.

"Yes, Prudence?" she said, approximately ten seconds later.

"It's about those clouds, Mrs. Edleman."

"The clouds? Prudence, are you delaying our field trip to ask about the weather?"

"Yeah." Why did Mrs. Edleman always feel the need to state the obvious? "They just look weird, don't they?

5

They're so dark. And the way they're acting, swirling over the house like that, it's almost like in a cartoon. I wonder if—"

"Prudence Potts, stop right there," Mrs. Edleman said, straightening her back and folding her hands over her belly. "Allow me to make certain things clear. First, the weather does not *act* in any way at all. The weather simply *is*. There is no conscious will behind it. Secondly, I cannot help but feel that you are setting the stage for another of your . . . investigations."

As her teacher frowned down the line at her, Pru thought about her most recent investigation, the one that Mrs. Edleman was no doubt referring to. Pru pictured the flyer she had posted around Middleton Elementary earlier that week. The top of the flyer had featured a blurry photo she had taken with her cell phone. The photo had shown a furry shape moving toward the teachers' parking lot. Below the photo had been the words:

SCHOOLYARD SASQUATCH

Enormous, lumbering, furry monster sighted by reliable witness yesterday in schoolyard. Students are warned to be on guard. Could this be the famous Bigfoot or Sasquatch? There is *no way* to be scientifically sure. But it probably is.

The flyer had earned Pru two weeks of detention, which struck her as completely unfair. How was *she* supposed to have known that Mrs. Edleman had just bought a new fur coat?

"Let me make one thing absolutely clear, Prudence. This is a field trip to learn about Viking explorers. There is nothing mysterious about the clouds in the sky, and there will be no investigations of any sort taking place here today." Mrs. Edleman returned her attention to the whole class. "Now, I trust that everyone understands my expectations. And remember, above all else, you are to stay together and not wander off. Is that understood?"

"Yes, Mrs. Edleman," the class chorused, and Pru chimed in.

Then she followed her teacher into the building and, first chance she got, wandered off.

✧

Winterhaven House perched high atop a rocky cliff overlooking the ocean to the east and the sleepy town of Middleton to the southwest. It was the oldest house in Middleton, and it belonged to the town's founding family, the Grimnirs. Old Man Grimnir lived there now.

It seemed like there had always been an Old Man Grimnir living there.

Everyone in Middleton knew that the town patron was fascinated with Viking history. He had even turned part of his vast home into a museum to showcase Viking artifacts. Some people said that Old Man Grimnir's fascination had begun years back when hikers found the remains of a centuries-old Viking camp in the woods that surrounded the town. Others said the family's interest in Vikings went back even further than that.

Some people whispered it went back *much* further than that.

Separated from her class, Pru walked past cases filled with swords and axes and strips of aged cloth. She saw maps and tapestries, and paintings of great ships with dragon-headed bows sailing off into the unknown.

Passing a window, Pru happened to glance at a squirrel sitting on a branch outside. It was a raggedy creature. Its bristled tail and the nick in its left ear suggested that this was a squirrel that had lived a bit and seen some things. Its eyes, small and black like polished stones, stared so intently at Pru that she felt for a moment as if she were herself an exhibit on display. Pru was relieved when the squirrel twitched its tail and bounded from the branch, leaving her to continue her exploration.

The exhibit rooms were small and cool and dimly

lit. They reminded Pru of basements, or caves, or other hidden places where secret things were kept, and sometimes found. In the last room she entered, Pru discovered a large glass display case. Inside the case rested a stone. It was a little larger than a dinner plate, and it was covered with strange writing.

She approached one of the signs set out for visitors. She had to squint to read it because the flickering fluorescent bulb above her made the room even darker than the others she had walked through. Shadows slid about. As her eyes adjusted, Pru read:

THE MIDDLETON STONE

Discovered by hikers in the woods around Middleton, the Middleton Stone is the pride of the Grimnir Collection. The runes on the stone, a form of Viking writing, tell the location of a powerful talisman called the Eye of Odin. Odin is described in stories as the Allfather of the Viking gods. The stone claims that the Eye is Odin's greatest treasure and his greatest torment. Unfortunately, many of the runes are of a unique style unfamiliar to modern archaeologists, so the specific location of the Eye of Odin remains lost to story and myth.

"Well, now," a voice directly behind Pru said, breaking the quiet. "Isn't that interesting?"

Pru spun about and took a few quick steps backward.

She tried to focus on the speaker who'd surprised her so. It took a moment. He was hard to see, at first, in the flickering light.

The man wore a long gray coat and gray hat. He was tall and thin, and his nose had achieved a level of prominence to which the other features on his face could only aspire. Pru thought it looked like just the sort of nose that would be perfect for sticking itself into places it did not belong.

"You startled me," Pru said. It was an automatic response, a phrase her mother often used. Pru felt silly for saying it, but it was true. She could have sworn she'd been alone in the room.

"I have a knack." A hint of a smile showed on the man's lips as he prowled around the display case, moving away from Pru. His eyes never left her. "You can hear me. And you can see me. That's interesting, too."

"Why would it be interesting that I can hear and see you?" It wasn't *that* dark in the room. And he'd been standing practically on top of her, apparently reading over her shoulder.

"Fair question," the man said, but he didn't answer it. Instead, he gestured with his chin to the Middleton Stone and the sign she'd read. "What do you make of that?"

"The stone? Who knows? It's just a story." She shrugged, reluctant to admit that the sign had piqued her curiosity.

The man's eyes flicked away from her for the first time, as though she no longer carried his interest. He looked disappointed. That upset Pru, though she could not have said why.

"There's no such thing as *just* a story," he said. "After all, we're all stories in the end. Sometimes, even, of our own telling. The trick is usually figuring out which bits of the story are true."

"Oh yeah? What's your story, then?" Pru asked, still smarting a bit from his dismissive tone.

The man stopped walking and returned his gaze to Pru. His long coat settled against his legs as he clasped his hands behind his back and looked directly at her from the opposite side of the case. The smile that had been playing about his lips returned and spread into a lopsided grin that showed his teeth but seemed to hide a great deal more.

"That's better!" The man in gray nodded his approval. "I like a person who knows how to ask a good question. I like such a person almost as much as someone who goes about trying to *answer* a good question. Still, as good as your question is, it's not the right one to ask, not quite. That is to say"—the man arched one brow—"I'd be willing to bet it's not the question that's been on your mind all morning."

Her hand shot to her messenger bag, slung over her shoulder. It held all her most important things (and her schoolbooks, when she was at school). That day, it carried something new—the card she had received that morning.

Pru didn't know what the question on the card meant. She didn't even know for sure where the card had come from. She had an idea, though. Or maybe it was a hope. Ideas were things people held in their heads, hopes the things they kept in their hearts. Hopes were secret, as far as Pru was concerned. So as her fingers found the card with its golden question, her eyes slid away from the man in gray.

"I don't know what you're talking about," she said.

Pru had the distinct impression the man in gray was laughing to himself. She could see it in his eyes. She could not, however, tell whether she was included in his silent laughter or whether she was the subject of it.

At that precise moment, the first clap of thunder rolled out from the clouds above. The whole room shook and the fluorescent light flickered out. The man in gray's voice whispered through the darkness.

It seemed to come from very close to Pru.

"You, my dear, are a natural-born fibber."

When the lights came back on a heartbeat later, the man in gray was gone.

CHAPTER 3

PRU HAD NEARLY FORGOTTEN ABOUT THE STRANGE weather by the time dusk temporarily masked the heavy clouds over Middleton. She'd even stopped thinking quite so much about her mysterious card. Her focus had shifted to the strange man she'd met in the shrouded rooms of Winterhaven House. Who was he? His long coat and hat reminded Pru of someone from the old-time detective movies she and her dad used to watch together.

The memory of curling up on the couch next to her dad caused Pru's chest to tighten. As she sat at her dining room table, she could hear her mother in the adjacent kitchen, washing the dinner plates by hand.

The dishwasher had broken the week before. It was the sort of thing Pru knew her dad would have fixed right away. Now, though, it sat untouched beneath the counter. It looked fine on the outside. Inside, it had gone all wrong.

Pru shifted her thoughts back to the man in gray. She couldn't shake the feeling that there was something decidedly detective-like about him. Perhaps that explained why she'd been more intrigued than creeped out by his strange behavior (and that he'd seemed to appear and vanish without a trace). There had been an air of familiarity about him.

"Mom?" Pru called into the kitchen.

A taller, older version of Pru appeared in the doorway a moment later. Anne Potts had shared all her most dramatic features with her daughter, including her red hair, small frame, and freckles. Pru thought those features combined into an effortless sort of beauty on her mother, whereas Pru just felt generally short and spotted.

"What is it, sweetie?" her mother asked, wiping her hands on a dish towel.

Pru rolled her pencil back and forth across the table and avoided her mother's eyes.

"Have they hired anyone new at the station?" Pru couldn't bring herself to ask the question that first sprang to her mind: *Have they replaced Dad?*

"I don't think so. But I can ask the next time I'm there, if you like."

"That's okay. It's nothing. I just thought I heard something about a new detective in town, that's all." Pru lifted her math book up so it covered her face.

"Pru." Her mother's voice went soft. Pru hated when her mother's voice went soft like that. "If it's something you'd like to talk about—"

"I have to do my homework."

Pru didn't look up over the edge of her math book to see her mother's reaction, but she heard it in the silence that filled the room. Eventually, that silence was broken by the sound of her mother's footsteps as she retreated into the kitchen. In her mind, Pru pictured her mother hanging the dish towel over the handle of the dishwasher. She found herself thinking once again of things that were all broken inside that no one knew how to fix.

✧

Pru awoke the next morning expecting more strange events. But even though a quick glance out her bedroom window revealed that the unusual clouds still hovered in the sky, Pru did not discover any more mysterious envelopes in her room or anywhere else in the house (she checked thoroughly). Nor did she encounter any tall men sporting a gray coat and hat, and with a pronounced nose on her walk to school.

She concluded (with some disappointment) that the weirdness of the day before had passed.

Even so, her arrival at school presented Pru with one surprise.

An unfamiliar boy stood at the front of the room by Mrs. Edleman's desk. He was just a bit taller than Pru, who everyone said was small for her age. He had a mess of blond hair and absolutely no freckles (which to Pru hardly seemed fair at all).

Pru studied the new kid from her seat. On the chest of his tie-dyed shirt he wore a name tag on which he had written "ABE," just like that. It seemed shouty, writing your name all in capitals. But nothing else about the new kid struck Pru as loud as Mrs. Edleman introduced him as their newest classmate. He shuffled awkwardly from foot to foot as he stood at the front of the class. When Mrs. Edleman said his name, he half raised his hand to wave, but then he seemed unsure if that was the right thing to do—and he ended up shoving both of his hands into the pockets of his cargo pants and looking down.

Pru almost felt bad for him.

Her sympathy quickly vanished when Mrs. Edleman partnered Pru and ABE on an assignment for their Viking unit so that ABE could catch up. Everyone else got to work alone. Not only did they have to read a Norse myth, which for some reason was the name for stories about Viking gods, goddesses, and heroes, but they also had to prepare a report on it to share with the class on Monday. A report already required far more schoolwork than Pru wanted to do over the weekend. Working with a partner would just make things more complicated.

Pru knew Mrs. Edleman had partnered them just to get back at her for wandering off at Winterhaven House the day before, but there was nothing she could do about it. So she sought ABE out at recess that day to figure out a time and place for them to meet.

She found him on the blacktop. He was standing apart from the other kids, hands in his pockets again, rolling a piece of sidewalk chalk beneath his feet. The chalk left marks on the broken pavement that reminded Pru of strange writing scratched on an ancient stone.

"So, I guess we should plan to meet and go over the story Mrs. Edleman assigned," Pru said as she walked up to ABE. No point beating around the bush.

"Okay, sure." ABE appeared pleased to have someone to talk to. "That would be great."

Pru did her best to ignore ABE's obvious relief at not being alone. It wasn't *her* job to help the new kid adjust, even if he did seem kind of lost.

"Well, we can't meet after school because I have detention this week and next." Pru folded her arms across her chest. "Here's a little hint for you. Don't compare Mrs. Edleman to a hairy, lumbering beast. She takes it all personal for some reason."

"Oh. Um . . . okay. Sure. I'll remember that. Thanks."

"Anyway, let's meet tomorrow. Do you know where the library is?" Pru knew ABE had just moved in, but Middleton was small and the library was hard to miss. It was also central enough that you could walk there from just about anywhere in town.

"Yeah. I saw it on my way in to school today. I've been wanting to go, actually."

"Okay, good. I'll see you tomorrow at eleven." With that, Pru walked off. It wouldn't do to be seen talking to a boy for too long. Sixth grade was weird. Everyone had come back from summer all filled with gossip about who wore what and who liked who. Pru didn't have any interest in that nonsense. She was better off with her investigations.

The thought made Pru glance upward. If she were to be completely honest—and complete honesty was something she tried to avoid, as a general rule—but if she *were* to be completely honest, she'd have to admit that she'd only mentioned the clouds to Mrs. Edleman the day before to get under her teacher's skin. But now the clouds really *did* seem ominous. They sealed the sky shut so that even though she was outside, she couldn't escape the sensation of feeling confined. It put her in mind of how she felt in the darkened hallways of Winterhaven House, with its hidden treasures and unexpected encounters.

She jumped at a sudden clap of thunder, then looked around quickly to make sure no one had seen her startled reaction. As she turned, she noticed the bushy tail of a squirrel as it darted from the playground area to the trees that bordered the schoolyard. Odd that a squirrel had come so close to where kids were playing.

Odder still that the squirrel seemed familiar, with its scruffy tail and the nick in its left ear.

CHAPTER 4

SATURDAY DAWNED GRAY AND GLOOMY AGAIN. PRU walked to the library. The dark clouds had spread as far across the sky as she could see. They left Pru feeling unsettled and anxious as she found ABE on the second floor. He was waiting with his books already open and spread before him.

"Hi," he said. He started to stand up.

Pru grunted something by way of a greeting before dropping into her seat. Deep down, she knew it wasn't really ABE's fault that they'd been assigned to work together. Mrs. Edleman wasn't there to be grouchy to, though, so accommodations had to be made.

ABE hovered over his seat a moment before settling

back down. "So, um, I guess maybe we should get started?"

"I guess." Pru hefted her messenger bag onto the table. "We should probably start with the story Mrs. Edleman assigned us."

"I actually read it last night. It was pretty good!"

"Are you kidding? You did homework on a Friday night? But that's the best night for TV."

"Oh. Actually, I don't really watch a lot of TV . . ." ABE abandoned the sentence. Perhaps he saw the look of astonishment on Pru's face. "Sorry. You're right, let's read the story."

With a roll of her eyes, Pru pulled out her own notebook and also began reading the Norse myth Mrs. Edleman had assigned.

THE STORY OF LOKI
AND THE BUILDING OF ASGARD'S WALL

Across the Rainbow Bridge lies the realm of Asgard, where the gods of the Vikings live.

In the early days, the city of the gods was vulnerable. It had no wall to protect it from the wild giants of nearby Jotunheim. Then one day a builder presented himself before Odin, Allfather of the gods.

"I will build your wall," the builder said, "and I will do it before two winters pass."

"For what price?" asked shrewd Odin, god of wisdom and war.

"I ask for the most beautiful goddess to be my wife, and I ask for the sun and the moon, too."

"Is that all?" mocked Odin. The other gods also raised their voices in outrage, all save one. Sly Loki appeared thoughtful.

"Give us a moment to consider your generous offer," Loki said, and he ushered the builder from the hall.

With their guest gone, the gods turned to the trickster. Though Loki was the blood brother of Odin, he was himself a child of giants and the other gods looked on him with suspicion. Loki, the Sly One, the Sky Traveler, the Shape-Shifter. He had always been different from them, even as a youth, with his clever mind and mischievous ways.

"What is in the twists and turns of your mind, Loki?" Odin demanded. "Would you give this stranger all the light, beauty, and warmth of the world?"

"I would not," Loki said. "But think! Suppose we accept this offer but demand that the task be done in just one winter, not two?"

"Impossible," the gods and goddesses exclaimed.

"Exactly. And if the builder fails in his task, then he gets no payment, none at all. So! We will have part of our wall built, at least, and at no cost."

Then the other gods congratulated Loki for his agile mind. They brought the builder back and Odin gave him the terms.

For his part, the builder demanded that if he must complete the job in so short a time, he should be allowed the aid of his stallion to help transport the stones for the wall.

"That was not in our bargain," said Odin. "It cannot be so."

"Odin, you are too stubborn," Loki interrupted. "Give him the use of his stallion. What harm can it do?"

In the end, Odin agreed, but later he warned Loki that the trickster would bear the consequences if his scheme went wrong.

The next day, the builder began his work and the gods retired to their own halls. As the wolves of winter howled, the gods remained in their warm homes and did not see the builder's progress. It would have brought them no joy if they had.

Each morning, the builder's stallion dragged great mountains of stone to the builder, who then cut, shaped, and placed the stones with a skill beyond any mortal. If the gods had seen him work, they would have known that the builder was a giant in disguise.

Three days before summer, the gods emerged from their halls and their feasting and stared in horror at the great wall surrounding their city. Only the gate remained unfinished, and it lacked just one stone!

The gods turned upon Loki, forgetting their earlier admiration. They told Loki that he had brought this woe upon them, and that he must fix things or face their wrath.

Loki fled the hall. When the gods followed him, they found not Loki outside but a beautiful mare.

The mare ran to the builder's stallion. With a toss of her mane, she led the stallion on a merry chase for three days. And for three days, the builder raged and cursed and searched for his stallion in the green fields and mountain paths, for he knew he could not move the final stone alone.

The first day of summer came, and the wall remained unfinished. The builder returned and demanded payment. He threw off his disguise and threatened to bring down the hall.

But by then the gods had guessed the builder's nature and had sent for Thor, the god of thunder *and their greatest warrior. Thor had been in the world of Midgard, where mortals live, for he was fond of mortals and was their protector.*

Thor had no love for giants, though, and they feared him greatly. When the giant rose up, Thor cast him down. Thor's fury roared like thunder, and the skies echoed his rage. Thor swung his hammer, and the giant fell.

Months later, Loki returned to Asgard. He brought with him a magnificent foal with eight legs, named Sleipner, which he gave to Odin. Odin was much pleased, and peace was restored to Asgard for a time.

"I don't get it," Pru said when she had finished. "Where did Loki get the baby horse?"

ABE's cheeks reddened. "Well, Odin did warn Loki that he'd *bear* the consequences if something went wrong."

It took a moment for Pru to understand the double meaning of the word. "Ew!" she exclaimed when she realized people could "bear" a child and that mares could "bear" a foal. ABE's blush deepened, but a moment later they both found themselves laughing.

Still laughing, Pru reached for her messenger bag to grab a pen. She accidentally grabbed the bag by the wrong end and spilled its contents onto the table and ground. Groaning, she retrieved her things from the floor and sat back up to gather what remained on the table. As she did, she saw that ABE held her special card.

"Hey, that's mine!" Pru yanked the card away. She'd still not had any luck puzzling out what "THE UNBELIEVABLE FIB" was, and she didn't know what the sender meant by *Be grave in your search, and avoid having stones in your head.* But it was still *her* card.

"Sorry." ABE instantly looked down. Whatever ease had begun to grow between them vanished. One of ABE's feet began to tap a nervous rhythm on the ground. "I didn't mean to. It's just, I really like riddles and stuff. They're one of the few things I'm good at. I'm kind of literal about things, and that helps with riddles. So I saw your card and I just . . . sorry."

"Never mind." Pru softened a bit. Most kids in her class just talked about how good they were at everything. ABE's attitude was refreshing.

"It's a good one, though. The riddle on the back of the card? I like it. Did you make it up? It took me a minute to figure it out."

"No, I didn't make it—wait." Pru stopped replacing items in her bag. "You know what the card means?"

"I think so. I mean, I don't know what 'THE UN-BELIEVABLE FIB' is. But I think I got the other part. It said to be 'grave,' right? And avoid 'stones in your head.' Well, headstones are what you put on actual graves, so I thought it must mean—"

"The cemetery." Pru leaned back in her chair and let her arms drop to her sides. How could she have missed that? It wasn't just a card she'd received.

It was an invitation.

Pru tried to ignore the flutter of hope that stirred in her chest. She had to answer the invitation, and she couldn't wait a moment longer. But she couldn't bring herself to go to the cemetery alone.

She glanced at ABE.

Her dad used to say that desperate times call for desperate measures. "Come on," Pru said, deciding. "We have to go."

CHAPTER 5

PRU ONCE READ A DESCRIPTION OF MIDDLETON IN A hiking guide (her dad had loved to hike). The guide had claimed that Middleton was aptly named, resting in the center of two extremes: wealth and power above, death below.

Pru had thought that description a little dramatic. Still, the guide was (technically) right. Middleton lay on an isolated stretch of the New England coast, surrounded on all sides by a heavy forest. The town itself lay midway up a hilled slope. At the crest of the slope, closest to the coast, sat Winterhaven House, enthroned on its high, hilly cliff. At the base of the slope lay Middleton Cemetery. Wealth and power above, death below.

The grounds that lay beyond the heavy iron gates of the cemetery were rolling and green, and Pru's dad was buried there.

She hated the place.

Mrs. Edleman had once explained that storms form because warm air rises and leaves an empty space for cold air to rush in—or something like that. Pru hadn't been listening too closely. Still, the idea had made some sense to her. Pru's dad's death the year before had left an empty place inside her. Sadness, anger, fear, and even resentment had filled the empty space and created a tempest of emotions. As a general rule, Pru avoided places that reminded her of death. This trip was necessary, though.

"Sorry, but can you explain it to me again?" ABE asked. He had to jog a bit to catch up to Pru, who was walking very fast. "Why exactly are we going to the cemetery?"

"Think of it like a game. The card is a clue, and now that we figured out what it means, we have to go where it tells us."

"Oh, okay." ABE nodded. Then, after a moment, he shook his head. "No . . . wait. I'm still not getting it. Why do we have to follow the clue? Who are we playing this game with?"

Pru didn't want to admit that she didn't quite know the answer to those questions. She also didn't want to think too hard about why it was so important to her to respond to the card's invitation.

If she did, she'd have to admit to herself that ever since her dad had died she had wanted to believe that his death wasn't real. She wanted to believe it was an "UNBELIEVABLE FIB."

Then the card had come and, now, the understanding that the card was inviting her to the cemetery. Despite her best efforts to stay calm, her mind conjured images of finding her dad there in the cemetery. He would confide in her that his death had been an elaborate ruse as part of a case he was working on— something involving mobsters, or government conspiracies, or parent-teacher conferences, or something equally evil. He would tell her he missed her too much to keep the lie going, so he'd sent the secret card to call her to him. She wasn't about to tell ABE all that, though.

"Look . . . either you want to come with me or you don't. It's up to you. But if you want to come, stop complaining." She set off at an even faster clip. A moment later, with a sigh, ABE followed.

There were two ways to reach the cemetery. They could either follow the main road downhill as it led through the woods to its main gates, or they could travel along the hiking trails that crisscrossed the forested area surrounding the town.

Because she was still supposed to be in the library for a while longer and didn't want to risk her mother seeing her walking along Main Street, Pru decided to follow the hiking trails. Her mom never hiked. There were ticks.

Pru led the way to the back of the library, where a break in the crumbling stone wall that surrounded the yard gave easy access to the woods beyond. A clap of thunder accompanied their entrance into the trees. Pru glanced up, grateful that the still heavy October foliage blocked out the view of the sky and the dark clouds overhead. The clouds had, if anything, grown darker since they had first appeared days before, and the thunder had grown more frequent.

It turned out that ABE had noticed the odd weather, too. "Does the sky seem strange to you?" he asked.

"Of course not." Pru tried to sound like the exact same thought had not just occurred to her. "It's just cloudy."

"I guess . . . Except, there's all that thunder. I mean, there's a *lot* of thunder."

"So? There's a storm coming."

"Yeah. It's just . . . thunder is the sound lightning makes, right?"

"So?"

"Well, I've been in your town for two days and it's been thundering pretty much nonstop the whole time.

But I've been looking and the thing is . . . the thing is, I haven't seen any lightning. None."

Pru's step faltered. The sky rumbled again, as though somehow it knew they were talking about it. She swallowed.

"You're just being paranoid. There's nothing strange about the sky. Nothing at all. Everything is absolutely, perfectly normal."

As it happened, it was immediately after Pru spoke those words that a somewhat shabby-looking squirrel with a small chunk missing from its left ear scampered to a low-lying tree branch just ahead and, quite unexpectedly, began to talk.

"I am the nigh omniscient Ratatosk," the squirrel said, demonstrating an impressive vocabulary, particularly for a squirrel. "And you two beardless, chittering simpletons shouldn't be here. No, no, no!"

The squirrel spoke in the quick, squeaky sort of voice one might expect a squirrel to use—if one were in the habit of expecting squirrels to speak.

"You're in extreme peril. Imminent jeopardy! Terrible danger, one might say." With that, the squirrel leapt to another branch and quickly disappeared from view.

Pru stared after it, speechless.

"Uh, Pru, did that squirrel just talk?" ABE said in a high-pitched voice that would trouble neighborhood dogs.

Pru's mouth worked, but she couldn't quite find any words.

ABE rambled on. "I'm pretty sure that squirrel just talked! Also . . . I think it insulted us."

Finally finding her voice again, Pru spun on ABE. "Did you do that? Because I've heard about ventriloquists, you know. I know how some people can throw their voice. If you're trying to make a fool out of me, I swear, I will kick you so hard." She meant it, too. Pru had a reputation. Everyone in her class knew: get Prudence Potts angry and nobody's shins were safe.

She was also pretty good with her elbows.

One look at ABE's face, however, told Pru that she could keep her elbows in reserve. He looked as shocked as she felt. As the squirrel's words sank in, Pru began to scan the woods around them. "Terrible danger," the squirrel had said.

"What do you think it meant?" she asked.

"Well, *nigh* means 'almost,' and *omniscient* means 'all-knowing,' so—"

"I meant about the *danger*, ABE! The *terrible danger*, remember?"

"Oh! Right, sorry!" ABE ran a hand through his hair. It appeared to be something he did when he was nervous. Pru began to understand why his hair always looked such a mess.

Before ABE could make any guesses as to what the

squirrel might have meant, the sound of splintering wood echoed through the trees, followed by a heavy crash. A flurry of motion in the distance caught Pru's eye. She looked in the direction of the movement and saw—

She wasn't sure what she saw.

She saw a tree fall. That much she knew. But, for just a moment, she thought she saw something else, too. Something big. Something really big.

The distance and the density of the trees made it difficult to see clearly, but the thing Pru saw looked like a man, only one who stood at least four times as tall as anyone she'd ever seen before. She only spied him for a moment, and then the figure disappeared behind a cluster of other trees and brush. Pru began backing away.

"ABE, I think we should keep moving."

ABE did not argue.

Branches blurred on either side of Pru as she and ABE turned and sped off. Pru's breath clouded before her. Distracted as she was by the inexplicable events that had occurred over the past few minutes, some part of her brain wondered about her clouded breath. It hadn't been that cold when they left the library, but there in the woods it felt like winter. Mist rose from the forest floor around and before them.

Pru heard the sound of footsteps behind her as the mist turned to a dense fog that enveloped her and

ABE. They were indeed the footsteps of something worrisomely big. The footsteps drew closer.

Pru had always heard people talk about fear like it was a cold thing. They got "chills," or became "frozen with terror." There in the woods, it occurred to Pru that fear wasn't always a cold thing. Sometimes, fear was a fire. A little spark could start it, and then it could grow to consume you and everyone around you.

Even in the sudden cold of the forest, fear burned in Pru. It consumed her and spread to ABE. Soon, they were running, sprinting, fast as they could through the trees. The mist made it difficult to see the ground, but they dodged roots and moss-covered stones as best they could.

The footsteps followed and Pru did not dare look back. She didn't have to. She could tell that whatever chased them was close.

ABE stumbled.

Pru watched in horror from the corner of her eye, praying that he'd regain his balance—but the stumble collapsed into a trip, and then ABE was on the ground.

Pru skidded to a halt. Purposely keeping her eyes on ABE (and not the woods behind him), she reached down and grabbed his jacket. Even as she did so, she could tell it was too late. She sensed something move nearby. She knew that if she just looked up, *it* would be there.

It was going to get her.

Before it could, though, the sky exploded.

The largest boom of thunder yet echoed across the heavens. Pru threw herself to the ground and covered her head. When she dared to look up, she saw that ABE had reacted the same way. She spun around, looking for whatever had been chasing them, sure that it must be right on top of them.

It wasn't.

Pru didn't understand. *Something* had chased them, something big and terrifying, and they'd been trapped. She was sure of it! Why did it turn away? Pru rose slowly and looked around again to be sure they were alone and to get a sense of where they were.

They had come to a stop in a dead section of the woods. Some past disease had robbed the surrounding trees of life and leaves so that the churning sky stood revealed above. The broken trees reminded Pru of a graveyard of ships. They rose from the misty ground like the masts of sunken vessels. Only jagged remains suggested there had once been branches on those wrecked trees, broken booms lost to some unknown storm.

"What just happened?" ABE asked, also rising to his feet and taking in their surroundings.

"I don't know." Pru was shaking. Her fingers slipped into her messenger bag where they brushed past the mysterious card and curled around her most prized possession, her dad's badge. She wished more than anything that he were there with her.

At that moment a man's voice made itself heard.

"Well, well," it said, coming from behind Pru. "Long time no see."

Pru's heart leapt cruelly toward hope. But even as she turned to face the speaker, recognition set in. Disappointment immediately followed.

It wasn't her dad speaking at all.

It was the man in gray.

CHAPTER 6

"WHERE DID YOU COME FROM?" PRU ASKED. SURPRISE roughened her words.

The man in gray leaned casually against a nearby tree. Mist swirled about his ankles and snaked up his legs. In his long coat and hat, he looked like an extension of the fog, as ghost-like and otherworldly as the landscape around them.

"I've been around. Why? Were you looking for me?"

"What? No. Listen." Pru shook her head and tried not to let her voice shake as the memory of her and ABE's flight through the woods returned. "There's something out there in the trees."

"Is that so?" The man in gray sounded relaxed, but

Pru noticed a spark of excitement in his eyes. She noticed something else, too. His nose began to twitch.

Taking a few steps in the direction Pru had indicated, the man reached into his coat's inner pocket. He withdrew what appeared to be a magnifying glass and held it before his eye as he gazed into the woods.

"Is this guy a friend of yours?" ABE whispered, edging closer to Pru.

"Hardly. He's some weirdo I met in the museum the other day."

"Oh. Okay."

ABE neither looked nor sounded reassured as the man in gray lowered his magnifying glass.

"Whatever was out there seems to be gone now. Did you happen to see what it was?" The man glanced back over his shoulder at Pru and ABE as he spoke. His voice remained casual, but Pru was sure of it now—his nose was definitely twitching.

"No, I . . . I only saw it from far away. But it was . . ." Pru faltered. She couldn't bring herself to describe what she had seen. Who would believe it?

"It was big," ABE said.

Pru wasn't sure whether she felt better or worse knowing that ABE had seen something, too.

"It was really, *really* big." ABE continued, "It was impossibly big."

"Was it? I'm sorry I missed that."

"You shouldn't be," ABE said, shaking his head.

"If you say so. Tell me, did you see anything else in the woods?"

Pru and ABE exchanged a look. Knowing how ridiculous it would sound, Pru willed ABE not to speak.

"Well . . . there was a, ah, squirrel," ABE said, swallowing.

"A squirrel? In the woods? That sounds normal enough."

"Not this squirrel."

"ABE . . ." Pru cautioned.

"It talked!" ABE continued, either not hearing her or unable to stop himself.

The lopsided grin and laughing eyes that Pru remembered from Winterhaven House returned. "Did it? A talking squirrel? Now, that is curious."

"He means it sounded like the squirrel talked," Pru interrupted. "*Someone* talked. It couldn't have really been the squirrel, obviously."

"Obviously," the man in gray agreed. "What did this talking squirrel of yours say?"

"He warned us of danger," ABE said. "And I'm pretty sure he insulted us."

"Is that so?" The man's nose, which had begun to quiet, resumed its twitching. "Now, that is *very* interesting. A talking squirrel is one thing, after all. But an *insulting* talking squirrel, that's something else."

"Enough about the squirrel," Pru said. She hated being laughed at, even if it was just with a look. "Who are you, anyway? What are you doing out here in the woods?"

"You can call me Mister Fox," the man in gray said.

"Is that your name?" ABE asked.

"*My* name? Of course not. What an absurd notion. No one can own a name. It's *a* name, though, and it's the one that suits me best. Now, as for what I'm doing here, I'm here in town precisely because there *is* something out there in the woods."

"Really?" Pru said. She'd nearly convinced herself that she'd imagined it.

"Of course. There have always been things in the woods." Mister Fox looked down his long nose at them. "But you knew that already. You've known for a long time. All children do. Think back to all those stories your parents told you when you were little about the things children find in the woods. Wolves. Witches. Giants."

Pru flinched at the mention of giants. "What have stories got to do with this?"

"Do you remember when you asked your parents if those stories were real—and don't deny asking. At

41

one time or another, in one way or another, every child asks if those stories are real. Do you remember what your parents said?"

"Yes," Pru said. "They said they were just pretend. They told the truth."

"Don't be so sure," Mister Fox said.

"They're just stories," Pru insisted.

"I believe we've discussed this already. There's no such thing as just stories."

"Are you saying that witches and . . . giants . . . are real?" ABE asked. "They can't be, though. Right? I mean, they're magic. Magic isn't real."

He glanced over his shoulder, back into the woods. "Is it?"

"I've traveled around a bit," Mister Fox answered, pushing back the tail of his long gray coat and then slipping his hands into his pockets. Most of the mist had lifted. What little remained seemed to cling to him as it swirled about his feet. "On one of my travels, I met an old woman. Interesting lady—bit of a strange fascination with chickens."

Pru blinked at the change of topic. She'd heard of trains of thought. Mister Fox's train seemed to have become derailed.

"But the strangest thing about the old woman was her ideas on magic," Mister Fox continued, getting his train back on track. "She had this notion that there were whole other worlds out there, worlds of magic. She told me that those worlds are connected to ours by avenues of possibility and perception and that, under just the right circumstances, creatures and beings from those worlds can come here."

"That's insane," Pru said.

Mister Fox laughed. "Says the girl who talks to squirrels."

"I didn't talk to the squirrel!" Pru answered. Before she could stop herself, she blurted, "The squirrel talked to me."

"And you didn't answer it? That seems just a bit rude. Is that the sort of person you are? Insane, and just a bit rude?"

Pru noticed ABE studying her. She fought the temptation to elbow him.

"Uh, could we get back to the part about magic being real?" ABE asked.

The man in gray approached ABE. He leaned forward, bending at the waist so he was nearly eye level with ABE. "And what sort of person are you, I wonder," he said.

Before ABE could answer, Pru stepped between him and Mister Fox. "This is ridiculous. There's nothing out there in the woods. I'm sure it was just our eyes playing tricks on us." She tried to sound confident.

"And our ears?" ABE asked, behind her.

Pru ignored him. "If magic was real, people would know. They'd see it. It would be on the news. You're not fooling anyone."

"Very few people can see it. You two, apparently, are among the few who can."

"I don't believe you."

"Of course you don't believe me. That's exactly how you know I'm telling you the truth."

"We're leaving," Pru said, shaking her head and trying to clear it of the crazy.

Mister Fox stretched his arm out. For a moment, Pru thought he might try to stop them. Instead, he rolled his hand in a gesture that they were free to go.

"I'd follow the main road back," he advised. "Best to avoid the woods for a bit."

Pru began walking away. ABE followed close behind.

"It's all about belief," Mister Fox called after them. "People believe too easily, today. When you believe in things, you close your mind to other possibilities. And magic is all about possibility. It's the ones who aren't sure what to believe who can see magic."

"Uh-huh, thanks," Pru called over her shoulder. But she turned to look back at him once more before leaving. Mister Fox had straightened. He stood with his hands in his pockets once more, watching them go.

"Be careful when you get back to town," he called.

"Things are happening here. You may think things look normal. *Don't be so sure.*"

Pru began to turn away. As she did, she noticed something she hadn't seen before, though she didn't understand how she could have missed it. Just a bit off to the side from Mister Fox stood an old shed of some sort. Or was it a small house? She wasn't sure. It hardly seemed important. She dismissed it from her thoughts—almost. It stayed with her in the quiet place in the back of the mind, the part where people keep things they are not sure of.

Ahead, Pru saw the manicured lawn of the cemetery peeking through the trees. With a start, she remembered the mysterious card and the reason for her and ABE's journey. Quick on the heels of the memory, however, came the realization that she was too tired to explore the cemetery. Her hope of finding her father there seemed foolish and distant to her now. Still, a part of her wondered what—or who—the clue might have led them to.

Lost in thought and not watching her step, Pru nearly tripped as her foot caught on something hard. She glanced down and was surprised to discover the crumbling remains of a chiseled gravestone lying flat on the ground.

They were in the cemetery already. It was clearly an

older section, partially reclaimed by the woods, where aged and crumbling headstones had already begun their own journey toward decay and dust. But the fact remained—they'd been in the cemetery all along.

Pru thought about the possible meaning of that as she and ABE entered the cemetery proper and left behind the older graveyard and the all-but-forgotten souls who dwelt within.

CHAPTER 7

EACH YEAR, MIDDLETON HELD AN EVENT CALLED the Explorers' Fair. People dressed as members of a Viking village, supposedly to celebrate the Vikings' extraordinary accomplishments as explorers. Pru's dad had always said that the real purpose of the fair was to humor Old Man Grimnir and his crazy Viking obsession so that he'd keep giving the town his money.

The fair was held on the grounds of Winterhaven House over Columbus Day weekend to draw attention to the fact that the Vikings traveled to North America long before Christopher Columbus made the journey. There were all kinds of Viking-related activities at the fair, like tying sailor's knots and archery competitions.

Pru had once suggested an axe-throwing contest, but no one had taken her seriously.

In addition to those other, non-axe-throwing activities, the Explorers' Fair also featured a number of booths set up to support the community. The Middleton Police Department, for example, always ran a canned food drive to help the hungry.

All sixth graders were expected to sign up to volunteer at one of the booths. The school called it a community service requirement. Pru called it child labor. Still, with the fair less than a week away, Mrs. Edleman's class lined up to walk down to the gym, where different organizations had set up tables to recruit volunteers.

Pru was grateful for the break from routine, and not just because it got her out of math (why would anyone even *want* to convert decimals to fractions?). It also gave her a chance to talk to ABE for the first time since their trip to the cemetery and their strange encounters with the squirrel, the thing in the woods, and the madman in gray—or Mister Fox, as he liked to be called.

He was *infuriating*, Pru decided. She carefully chose a word she knew well, mostly because people (Mrs. Edleman in particular) would often use it to refer to her. But Mister Fox really *was* infuriating. He was always saying things that didn't make sense and laughing with his eyes. And that stupid, lopsided grin! Pru resolved not to give him another thought.

She wondered if she'd see him again.

Then she resolved *really* not to give him another thought.

Pru navigated the gym until she found ABE in front of a table with a banner that read *The Earth Center.* Pru had heard of it. It was Middleton's environmental organization. From what she could see from the flyers on the table, the group planned to organize a recycling drive. ABE held the sign-up sheet in his hands as Pru approached.

"ABE, that's perfect!"

"Really?" ABE beamed. "Thanks. I think so, too. I mean, we throw away so much stuff that we shouldn't. A recycling drive is a great way to draw attention to that and—"

"Yeah," Pru interrupted, stepping closer to ABE and taking the clipboard from him. "My thoughts exactly. Also, it's totally an excuse to go sneaking around town investigating."

"Right, and . . . wait. What? Investigating what?" ABE looked at her with raised eyebrows.

"Shh." Pru gestured at ABE to keep his voice down. "Something weird is going on in this town, and you know it. The squirrel? The thing in the woods?"

"But you said we just imagined those things."

"So? I say things. It's what people do. They say stuff. That doesn't mean you should believe them. Trust me."

"Oh. Okay. Wait . . . am I supposed to believe you now?"

"Obviously! Look, the point is that something strange is happening. I'm not saying for sure that I think the squirrel talked or that I saw . . . anything . . . in the woods. Those could have been tricks or something." They'd seemed so real at the time, but how could they have been? "There's other stuff. Trust me, someone needs to investigate. And looking for recyclables for a couple of hours after school is the perfect excuse to snoop around town."

Pru picked up the pen attached to the clipboard by a worn string and started to write her name. Her hand paused midway through writing the *r*, however, as she noticed the name that occupied the line above. Aloysius B. Evans.

"*Alloy-see-us?* That's your real name?"

"It's pronounced Al-oh-ISH-us," ABE corrected, looking down. His face turned as red as Pru's hair as he added, "It means 'famous warrior.'"

"Famous warrior?" Pru tried not to laugh. She failed miserably.

"I didn't name myself."

"It's not that bad," Pru said, seeing how upset ABE looked. "Really. Scout's honor."

"You were a Scout?" ABE looked up, surprised.

"Well, no. Not exactly. But it's the thought that counts, right?" Pru tilted her head, remembering the first time she saw ABE. "Wait a second. So that's why you wrote ABE in all capitals on your name tag, isn't it? Because *A*, *B*, and *E* are your initials. But if you don't like your first name, how come you don't just go by your middle name? Lots of kids do that."

"It's Bartholomew."

"Oh." Pru didn't have to say anything more. Bartholomew got shortened to Bart, and everyone knew what *Bart* rhymed with. ABE looked so miserable that Pru took pity on him. "Well, it could be worse. Your name's better than Prudence, at least."

"What's wrong with Prudence?"

"Are you kidding? It's bad enough it sounds like an old lady's name. But do you even know what *Prudence* means?"

Pru wished she could take the question back as soon as she asked it. She'd learned in the woods that asking ABE if he knew what a word meant was like asking Mrs. Edleman if she liked giving kids detention.

"It means using good judgment to plan for the future, right?"

"See?" Pru's face darkened. "It's a stupid name.

You can't plan for the future. Things just happen. Terrible things, and you can't see them coming or stop them. People die, even. And you can't know. You can't. Anything is possible. I *hate* my name."

ABE opened his mouth to say something, but no words came out. Instead, another voice made itself heard.

"Oh my, how familiar that sounds."

Startled, Pru looked up to see an older woman standing behind the Earth Center's table. She hadn't been there when Pru first approached ABE. Pru figured she must have stepped up, unnoticed, while they were talking.

The woman had the sort of face that made Pru immediately think she was someone's mother, or possibly someone's grandmother (it was also the sort of face that made it hard to judge her age). Even though it was October, the woman wore a long, flowing dress and sandals. She looked nice enough, Pru supposed. Actually, at second glance, Pru thought she looked annoyingly nice. She was gazing at Pru with her hands clasped over her heart and a "Let's talk" expression on her face.

Definitely someone's mother.

"I'm Fay Loningtime. And I feel your pain, little girl. Oh, how I hated my name when I was your age." Pru flexed her elbows at the "little girl" comment that followed the woman's introduction, but curiosity got the better of her.

"What's wrong with your name? Fay doesn't sound *too* bad."

"I suppose it wouldn't seem so to you. But where I grew up, I was very different from those around me. Some things that were very easy for my peers were difficult for me. They delighted in teasing me and making up names for me."

"Like what?" Pru asked. She tried not to sound too curious.

"Well, for example, they called me 'Fay Long-in-time' because I was never quite as fast as them, or as strong." Fay sighed, and the fingers of one hand fluttered over her heart. "But we outgrow such things, don't we? Still, do you know what I did when my name bothered me most? I made a game out of it. Shall I show you?"

Pru shrugged. It was still better than math. Fay turned to the table to grab a pen and piece of paper. She wrote her full name: FAY LONINGTIME.

"First, I would write my name. Then I would rearrange the letters to try and make new words or phrases. It always excited me to find one. I pretended each new word or phrase was a secret message written just for me, revealing hidden truths about myself. Would you like to see my favorite?"

"I would," ABE said. Pru rolled her eyes at ABE's eagerness for another riddle.

One at a time, Fay crossed out the letters of her name and rewrote them in a different order until they spelled FLY INTO ENIGMA.

"Do you know what an enigma is?" Fay asked.

"It's another word for a riddle, or mystery," ABE-the-walking-dictionary answered.

"Exactly. I liked it because it seemed to tell me to seek mystery and adventure in life. I happen to think that's good advice for anyone, young or old."

Pru looked up at that. Anyone who liked mysteries couldn't be *all* bad.

A shuffling of bodies around her drew Pru's attention to the front of the gym. Mrs. Edleman stood there, summoning her students back into line.

"Well, okay, thanks. But we've got to go," Pru said, grabbing ABE's arm.

"No, thank *you*. It warms my heart to see you children getting involved in helping your world. Welcome to the Earth Center. Go now and seek your own mysteries. Fly into enigma!" Fay thrust one hand into the air in an enthusiastic gesture as Pru led ABE quickly away.

"And we're going to have to see her every day for community service," Pru muttered to ABE as they lined up. Still, it would be worth it for an excuse to explore the town.

And Pru knew just where to start their explorations that very afternoon. She wasn't ready to go back to the cemetery—the fear she'd felt in the woods had been too real. But her dad wouldn't have turned his back on an investigation, and neither would she.

Luckily, there was another option. Every strange thing that had happened so far had started the morning of the class trip to Winterhaven House. That was where she first met Mister Fox, too. Pru had no idea what was going on in Middleton, but there was one thing she *was* sure of.

A place as big as Winterhaven House had to have plenty of recyclables.

CHAPTER 8

WINTERHAVEN HOUSE ROSE UP FROM THE CLIFF TOP and imposed its presence on the blotted skies. The wind whipped Pru's hair about her face, and thunder boomed as she and ABE stood outside the gates of the mansion that afternoon.

"So, ah, remind me why you wanted to come here, again?" ABE said.

"It all started here." Pru combed the hair from her eyes. "That card you saw in the library? The one that led us to the cemetery? It appeared in my house the same morning our class had a field trip here. That was the day before you started school."

"It just appeared in your house?"

Pru nodded. "Weird, right? That was the same

morning all this strange weather started. And then we got here to Winterhaven House and I"—Pru cleared her throat—"accidentally got separated from the class. That's when I met Mister Fox for the first time."

"He was here? Okay, that does sound like a lot of coincidences. I can see why you might want to, ah, investigate here." ABE lowered his voice as Pru turned to face the mansion. "Now I just wish someone would explain to me what *I'm* doing here."

Perhaps the wind carried ABE's words, or perhaps he spoke louder than he'd meant to, but Pru heard his muttered comment and turned back to face him.

"Actually I was kind of wondering that, too," Pru said. She'd met him at the Earth Center after her detention and, a bit to her surprise, managed to persuade him to go with her to Winterhaven House. Other people didn't usually show much interest in her investigations, unless it was to tell her to stop one. "Why did you decide to come?"

"I'm not sure, I guess. I mean . . . I'm curious. *Something* strange happened in those woods over the weekend. So I kind of want to know what's going on. Also, you're, ah, basically the only kid in school who's talked to me."

Pru had to smile at that. "Well, anyway, come on. I can show you where I first met Mister Fox."

She led ABE into the museum wing and past

bored-looking docents in red vests and badges that expressed far more welcome than the volunteers themselves. She did her best to retrace her route to the room with the Middleton Stone. When she found it, she stepped back and let ABE read the sign in front of the exhibit, just as she had done.

"So this stone is like a treasure map to something called the Eye of Odin?" ABE said when he had finished. "That's kind of cool. I wonder what 'the Eye' is, really. And I wonder how it could be Odin's greatest treasure and his greatest torment."

"I don't know. Wait a minute." Pru frowned as she considered a piece of information she hadn't had on her last visit. "Odin? I know that name. He was in that story we read, wasn't he?"

"Yeah. He's like the head of the Norse gods. I mean, it's just a story, obviously, but I wonder if the Eye of Odin was a real thing that got named after him."

"Just a story." The words rang in Pru's ears. "There's no such thing as 'just a story,'" she muttered. She shot a glance at ABE to see if he'd heard her, but he appeared distracted by another exhibit in a corner of the room.

"Pru, did you see this?"

Set back in a shadowed corner of the room was another glass-enclosed exhibit. Pru must have been too distracted by Mister Fox on her first visit to notice it.

"No way," Pru said when she stepped up beside

ABE and peered through the glass. Inside was a life-size model of a squirrel. Pru read the sign on the front of the case.

RATATOSK THE MESSENGER

There are three worlds in Norse mythology. Asgard is the world of the gods. Midgard is the world of mortals. Niflheim is the world of the dead. A giant ash tree called Yggdrasil connects the three worlds. Many animals make Yggdrasil their home. One of those animals is Ratatosk, the squirrel. Ratatosk often serves as a messenger in the myths. He carries insults back and forth between an eagle at the top of the tree and a dragon at the bottom. Ratatosk also carries messages for the gods. Because of the ease with which he travels between worlds and the messages he carries, Ratatosk often knows more of the affairs of the gods than even they suspect.

"*No way,*" Pru repeated. "According to this, Ratatosk was a talking insult squirrel."

"It's got to be a joke, right? Do you think that guy, that Mister Fox, could be playing a trick on us? He was here in this room with you that other time. Maybe he saw this and—" ABE stopped suddenly as a small rustling noise came from the opposite side of the room, close to the door.

Pru and ABE exchanged a glance and then, slowly,

edged their way around the exhibit of the Middleton Stone that stood in the center of the room. Together, they peered around the corner of the exhibit toward the doorway. At first, it looked empty.

Then they looked down.

Standing on its hind legs in the center of the doorway was a small gray squirrel. His tail looked a bit worse for wear, and his left ear had a small tear in it.

Pru and ABE looked at the squirrel.

The squirrel looked at Pru and ABE.

He winked.

Then, he turned tail and ran.

Pru hesitated only a second before shouting, "Get it!" and taking off in pursuit.

"What? Pru, wait!"

"I want answers," Pru yelled back over her shoulder. She ran as fast as she could manage in the packed exhibit rooms and halls. The squirrel had a much easier time of it as he scampered under glass exhibit cases and along woven tapestries.

At one point, the squirrel's flight forced Pru to take a corner sharply—too sharply. She managed (barely) to avoid bumping into a tall, narrow pedestal that displayed an old earthen jar. But her messenger bag swung out and caught the corner of the display.

Pru didn't stop. She did look back, though, just in

time to see ABE slide on his knees to catch the falling artifact.

The squirrel led Pru into a hallway that ended at a closed door. She had him!

Triumph turned into doubt, however, when Pru noticed that the door had a narrow, rectangular window at the top that had been opened to allow air to pass through. Pru whispered a silent prayer that it was not open wide enough for the squirrel to fit through.

It was.

The squirrel scampered up the wooden doorframe with ease and leapt through the window. Just before he did, however, Pru saw him turn his little squirrel head to her *and stick out his tongue.*

"Rudest. Squirrel. Ever," Pru said through clenched teeth as she sprinted for the door.

"Pru, wait!" ABE called from behind. "You can't!"

Pru hadn't even been aware that ABE had caught up again, but she ignored his warning and opened the door, and then raced through. On the other side, Pru found that the squirrel had increased his lead. She chased him, and ABE's footfalls soon sounded once again behind her.

The hallway around Pru widened and became far less cluttered, but she remained focused on the chase and hardly noticed. After a final turn around a corner,

Pru entered a large open space. The squirrel was no-where to be seen.

ABE came up behind her, breathing heavily. He looked nervous. Well, he looked more nervous than usual, anyway.

"Pru, we have to go back," he said between breaths.

"Why? Where are we, anyway?" She didn't remem-ber this part of the museum. The room they stood in was huge. Various figures and creatures were carved into the granite walls around her. Fierce Viking war-riors brandished swords at beasts of every sort, though most often their opponents were giants and serpents and wolves, everywhere wolves. The figures marched along the walls. They prowled around corners and slithered over archways, recurring often enough in dif-ferent configurations that Pru sensed there was a spe-cific tale unfolding before her. From what she could tell, the story told by the figures stretched out into other parts of the building. Pru wondered what chap-ters waited in unexplored rooms.

It took a moment for Pru to see that there weren't any exhibit cases in the room. Nothing was labeled, as it had been elsewhere in the museum. All in all, it looked more like someone's house than a museum.

"Uh-oh," she said.

"Didn't you see the sign on the door you went through?" ABE's eyes darted from one spot in the room to another. "The one that said DO NOT ENTER in big black letters? We're not in the museum anymore. We're in Mr. Grimnir's *house*."

"It's not my fault. The door wasn't locked! Why wouldn't they lock the door?" Pru glanced around, trying to figure out the way they'd come. There were three hallways leading from the room. "Do you remember the way back?"

"I'm not sure. All the hallways look alike."

"I'm really starting to hate that squirrel," Pru muttered. "Come on. I think it's this way."

"Are you sure?"

"Absolutely."

She wasn't sure at all.

ABE was right. All the halls looked exactly alike. Pru quickened her step, but she soon became certain she'd chosen the wrong direction and would have to go back. Before Pru could say anything, however, a sound reached her that made her freeze. She grabbed ABE's arm and raised a finger to her lips. After a moment ABE's eyes widened. He heard it, too.

Footsteps echoed down the hall from the direction Pru and ABE had come, and they were getting louder. Pru took some comfort in the fact that they sounded like the footsteps of a normal-sized person. It was a small comfort, though. She and ABE were, technically, breaking and entering. She didn't care to think about how many weeks of detention and grounding she would get if they were caught.

A small door stood nearby. Pru pulled on its handle, hoping that unlocked doors were the rule in Winterhaven House. It turned out they were. The door opened to reveal a small broom closet. Pru yanked ABE inside. She had to fight the urge to slam the door shut, but she took some pride in the soft *click* as it finally settled into place. Closing a door quietly was another detective skill she'd practiced (the trick was keeping the knob turned until the door was shut, so the latch wouldn't make much noise).

Huddled in the dark, Pru felt a gossamer thread brush against her cheek. It made her think of spiderwebs, and then of spiders, and she had to clench her teeth and tighten her fists to keep still. The sound of ABE's quick breathing was surprisingly comforting.

They'd be fine. Whoever was coming would pass them by, and then she and ABE could slip back out the way they'd come and try another hallway. Pru listened as the footsteps got closer and closer. Then they stopped.

They stopped right outside the door.

Pru held her breath and willed the person to just keep walking. The closet was empty. There was nothing in it at all that anyone could want!

Except for them.

The door opened, revealing a tall, young-looking woman with a severe expression. Her blonde hair hung to her waist in a long, heavy braid. She did not appear at all startled to see them there, which surprised Pru quite a bit.

"You will both come with me," the woman said, studying them with sharp blue eyes.

Pru swallowed, feverishly trying to come up with a perfectly good reason why she and ABE might be hiding in the closet of the house of the richest man in town. She would have preferred a reason that made no mention of a talking squirrel. Before she could think of anything to say, the woman spoke again and her words so astonished Pru that her mind went blank.

"I'm Hilde," the woman said. "I'm to take you to Mr. Grimnir. He has been expecting you."

CHAPTER 9

AS PRU AND ABE FOLLOWED HILDE, PRU SAW THAT the figures on the walls did extend into other parts of the building. Warriors and creatures of stone flowed through the halls of Winterhaven House in a frozen tableau. Every so often, a shifting shadow would create the impression that the figures weren't still at all but were moving at an excruciatingly slow pace.

"It's like a story, written in stone," ABE said, also studying the figures as they walked.

"All stories are written in stone," the woman said. Her voice was grim.

"We didn't do anything wrong, you know," Pru said to their escort, turning her attention from the building's architecture. "The door wasn't locked."

"Are we in trouble?" ABE asked.

"Mr. Grimnir has been expecting you," Hilde repeated. She sounded a little like Pru's aunt who lived in Minnesota. "Whether you are in trouble remains to be seen."

"But that doesn't even make any sense," Pru said. "How could he be expecting us? *We* didn't even know we were coming here."

"Mr. Grimnir does not trouble himself with all the many things that other people do not know."

Hilde led Pru and ABE to a large rectangular room on the main floor of the house. A long wooden table ran the length of the room, with benches to either side. A fire burned in a hearth at the far end, and someone had placed a high-backed chair before the fire. The chair was big and wooden. Even at a distance, Pru could see that it was elaborately carved. It reminded her of a throne. The chair faced the fire, so Pru could not see for sure if there was anyone seated in it.

"Go on. He doesn't like waiting," Hilde said, gesturing to the chair.

Pru began walking toward the chair and ABE followed behind her, so close he stepped on her heel a time or two. As they rounded the table and walked along the far wall, they passed a series of long, pointed windows like Pru had seen in pictures of castles. Outside, rolls of

67

thunder crashed against the walls of the stone mansion like waves against a rocky shore.

Glancing through one window, Pru saw that the clouds in the sky seemed to be darkest above the mansion, almost as black as night. The fire offered the room's only light, so even though it was daytime, the room remained dark.

Stepping close to the chair, Pru noticed a wide-brimmed hat hanging over its back. In a nearby corner stood a tall walking stick, knotted and worn.

"You've finally arrived, I see."

The voice that came from behind the chair was old and deep, and sounded like rocks rolling down a mountainside.

Pru cleared her throat. She didn't understand why Old Man Grimnir didn't sound mad that they'd been caught in his house, but Pru wasn't about to look a gift horse in the mouth. She also didn't understand why everyone kept acting like Pru and ABE had been expected. Maybe the old man was crazy? Pru figured that could be a help. It would make it easier for her to talk their way out of this. It would be like trying to talk her way out of trouble with Mrs. Edleman, something with which she'd had lots of practice (if not as much success as she'd have liked).

"Hi. Old Man . . . um, I mean, *Mr.* Grimnir." Pru

had to clear her throat again. She didn't like how shaky her voice sounded. "Look, we're sorry we came into your house. It was an accident. You *should* lock your doors, you know. We weren't trying to cause any trouble, or anything."

"No? Well, that's a comfort. One mischief-maker is enough to deal with." A snort of laughter followed the old man's comment.

Pru edged forward just a bit more until she could make out some of Mr. Grimnir's profile from where she stood. She saw thick white hair, a full beard, and a hooked nose that looked like it had been broken in some past scuffle. His skin had the fine sort of wrinkles you would find on a once-rolled bit of tinfoil that someone had tried to flatten smooth again but couldn't quite.

"What brought you to my home?" Old Man Grimnir said. "And speak truthfully. I've dealt with far better liars in my day than either of you could hope to be."

"We were looking for recyclables," Pru said.

The old man was silent.

"Also, we, ah, came to see the Middleton Stone," she added.

"I see. Well, you are not the first ones to find the stone interesting. Others before you have sought the treasure it points to. Tell me, do you know the story of the Eye of Odin?"

"No," ABE said. Pru could hear the enthusiasm in his voice. He was probably hoping Old Man Grimnir would give him a book about it or something.

"Not many do. It is an old story. Listen." The firelight showed red on the old man's beard and cheek as he settled deeper into his chair.

Pru couldn't believe their luck. Were they really going to get let off with just a story?

"The tale begins in the hall of Valaskjalf—" he pronounced it Val-ask-chalv—"Odin's home in high Asgard. From Valaskjalf, Odin saw all that happened in the three worlds."

Pru remembered the three worlds mentioned in Ratatosk's exhibit. Asgard had been the home of the gods, if she remembered right.

"Odin sat with his son, Thor. Thor could see that his father was troubled. When Thor asked about the reason for his father's unhappiness, Odin answered that he thirsted for knowledge.

"Thor himself rarely bothered with thinking," Old Man Grimnir said with contempt. "So he could not understand his father's desire. He reminded his father that from his high seat, he could see everything. Odin knew all that happened as it happened. It was enough knowledge for anyone, Thor insisted.

"Odin replied it was not enough.

"And so Thor reminded his father that he had two ravens, Thought and Memory. They whispered in his ear each night of all they had seen that day, and all they remembered of days gone by. So Odin knew all that happened as it happened, and he knew all that had happened in times past. It was enough, Thor insisted.

"Odin replied that it was not enough."

"What else is there?" Pru asked.

"Thor asked Odin the very same question. That is when Odin told Thor of Mimir, who guards the Well of Wisdom. One sip from the well would give Odin the power to see the future. He would see all that would happen in all the days to come."

Old Man Grimnir paused for a moment in his telling. As he did, a shade of darker black broke from the charcoal sky outside Winterhaven House and hurled itself against the glass of a nearby window with a terrible *ca-caaaww*. Pru jumped as a raven clamored against the window in a riot of beating wings and scratching talons.

"Begone, blood-swan pest!" Old Man Grimnir shouted. "And I'll hear nothing from you, either."

Pru blinked, thinking the old man was speaking to ABE and her. Then a soft flutter of wings from above alerted Pru to the presence of another raven, twin to the first, perched in the beams overhead.

Two ravens.

Pru tried to catch ABE's eye, but he appeared intent on Old Man Grimnir and the story.

"Where was I?" Old Man Grimnir grumbled.

"You were talking about Mimir, the guardian of the Well of Wisdom," ABE said in hushed tones.

"Ah, yes. Thor did not take his father's words well. He knew of Mimir and he knew Mimir took his role as guardian seriously. Thor reminded Odin that Mimir challenged anyone who tried to drink from the well to a battle of wits. Each contestant had to wager something most would not gamble with."

"What did they have to wager?" Pru asked.

"His own head," Old Man Grimnir said. ABE gulped as the old man continued. "But Odin would not be denied. He set off for the Well of Wisdom. He left behind his golden helm and spear and his eight-legged steed, Sleipnir. He went in the guise of a humble mortal traveler, taking only a walking stick and a wide-brimmed hat to cover his face, and Mimir did not know him."

"Mimir couldn't have been too great a guardian if he got tricked by such an easy disguise," Pru said.

"Do you think not? Mimir was farseeing. Next time you are at a beach, look out and try to see every grain of sand at once. Odin's disguise was enough to discourage Mimir's focus, and so he welcomed the traveler.

When Odin asked for a sip from Mimir's spring, the guardian told Odin of the contest he must win in order to drink. Each would ask the other three questions. If either one failed to answer a question, his head would be forfeit. Odin agreed."

Warmed by the flickering firelight, Pru found herself wrapped in Old Man Grimnir's story and carried off into his other world of warrior gods and magical springs.

"Mimir asked his questions, each one more difficult than the last. But Odin had seen much, and all that the gods knew, he knew. He answered first one question, then the next, then the next. Only then did Mimir know the traveler for who he was, for no one but Odin was wise enough to best the guardian. Mimir welcomed Odin as Allfather, and invited him to ask his three questions.

"But wise Odin had just one."

Old Man Grimnir paused again and stared into the fire. When the silence stretched longer than Pru could take, she asked, "What? What was Odin's question?"

As if he had been waiting for the prompt, Old Man Grimnir exhaled in a long, slow breath.

"Odin knew all things had their price. So he asked the only question that mattered: 'What price would you accept for a drink from your spring?'"

Beside her, Pru heard ABE let out a slow breath.

Old Man Grimnir must have heard, too, because he paused yet again.

"What?" Pru asked.

"Odin's question," ABE said. "It was really smart. If Mimir didn't answer it, he'd lose his head. So Odin was sure to get what he wanted."

"So it was. Mimir knew he had been tricked and beaten. But he would take his payment. The price he claimed was sight for sight. For a drink from the Well of Wisdom, he would take Odin's right eye."

"Wait! You mean he had to take out his own eye?" Pru tried to imagine what that would be like. Her body shivered involuntarily. She couldn't think of anything that would be worth that.

Old Man Grimnir ignored the question. "Odin would not be discouraged. He feared nothing, so he took his prize. He drank from the Well of Wisdom and watched as images of days to come filled his mind. He watched until he could no longer tell whether the images in his head were visions of the future or memories of the past. Then Odin saw the most terrible of sights."

Outside, the raven in the window let out a cry. Old Man Grimnir dug his nails into the wooden arms of his chair.

"Odin saw Ragnarok," he continued. "He saw that one day there would be a great war between the gods of Asgard and the giants of Jotunheim. That war, which would be called Ragnarok, would destroy both races and leave all in ruin.

"It was too much to see, too much to know, even for the Allfather. He tore his right eye from his head in payment and hurled it into the spring, closing his one remaining eye. He stood there, longing for blindness, for uncounted days. In time, the other gods sought out Odin and begged him to return to Asgard. Only sly Loki held his tongue, his attention caught by a small round object that looked up at him from the bottom of the Well of Wisdom."

"He saw the Eye?" Pru asked.

"He did. The Eye of Odin lay almost forgotten at the bottom of the well, where Mimir had left it. But Odin knew it would not stay forgotten."

"Why?" Pru asked. "Who would want a torn-out eye?"

"The eyes of gods are not like the eyes of men," Old Man Grimnir answered. "Though Odin could no longer see from it, the Eye was not blind. It still held all the visions Odin had seen. Do you understand?"

"Are you saying that anyone who looked into the Eye of Odin would see the future?" ABE asked.

"Just so. Understanding the burden such knowledge held, Odin bargained with Mimir so that the Allfather could hide the Eye from mortal and god alike. Mimir agreed—he had no care for the Eye itself. He had only taken it to spite the Allfather. So Odin took the Eye and hid it. Then Odin wrote its secret location on a great rune stone. He hid the stone somewhere in the three worlds and returned home, there to wait through the long days until Ragnarok, his thirst for knowledge quenched at last."

"Wait," Pru said after a moment, frowning. "That ending doesn't make sense. If Odin didn't want anyone to find the Eye, why would he write down where he hid it?"

At first, Old Man Grimnir did not reply. Then, ever so slowly, he turned his head just enough so that the line of shadow shifted across his face and gave Pru her first full look at their host.

Her breath caught and she took a startled step back.

"Who can say?" Old Man Grimnir answered. "Perhaps Odin had foreseen a day when the Eye would be needed. Who can know the mind of a god?"

Pru didn't answer. She couldn't. Shock silenced her. Because when the owner of Winterhaven House turned around, Pru saw something astonishing.

Old Man Grimnir was missing one eye.

CHAPTER 10

AS SOON AS HILDE ESCORTED PRU AND ABE FROM Winterhaven House, Pru began running. She ran until her sides ached and her breath came in short, ragged bursts expelled from between reddened cheeks. ABE ran alongside her. They'd traveled half the distance down the main road that connected Middleton and Winterhaven House when they finally stopped.

"Pru! His eye! Did you see?" ABE said between gasps.

Pru placed her hands on her hips and leaned her head back to catch her breath.

"I saw. It was kind of hard to miss."

"He had one eye. And two ravens!"

"I noticed that, too." What did it mean? Pru was glad when ABE fell silent for a moment. She needed a second to gather her thoughts and catch her breath. ABE's next question robbed her of both, though.

"Pru?" ABE's voice dropped to a whisper. "What . . . what did *you* see in the woods that day?"

Pru looked at ABE. His head was ducked, but he was looking at her from beneath his lowered brow. She didn't have to ask what day he was talking about. Above them, the dark clouds rolled like the surface of a sea that linked them to some distant, unknown shore. Thunder rumbled in the distance.

They'd never actually talked about what happened in the woods and what they'd seen, not really. They'd talked about the squirrel a bit because squirrels seemed harmless—even talking ones.

But the other thing in the woods? The thing that had chased them? That hadn't felt harmless. So they'd talked around it instead of about it. They'd used words like "something" and "big." But it hadn't just been something big.

"It was a giant," Pru said. "That's what I saw. I mean, it couldn't have been. I know it couldn't have been. It had to be an illusion, you know? Like when you think you see a face in a tree. But in the woods that day, I thought I saw a giant."

Pru wrapped her arms about herself as a cool

breeze blew through, carrying with it the scent of the ocean.

"That's what I saw, too," ABE said.

They stood together a moment in the silence of shared discovery and disbelief.

"Pru," ABE finally said, "how come your town has talking squirrels and old men with one eye and two ravens and . . . and giants?"

"I don't know, ABE. I really don't. But I think we both know who might be able to answer your question."

"Mister Fox," ABE said.

He did not sound happy.

☆

Sitting at her dining room table that night, Pru thought about talking squirrels, things in the woods, old men with just one eye, and strangers with mischievous grins. She tried to find a place for all those things in the world she knew and understood, only they just wouldn't fit.

It was a little exciting.

It was also scary.

The familiar sounds of her mother in the kitchen comforted Pru. She allowed herself to be soothed by the opening of doors and the rattling of dishes as the dinner plates were returned to the cabinet.

On a whim, Pru pulled out the mysterious envelope and the even more mysterious card that lay inside.

Everything strange that had happened had begun with the envelope's arrival. It had appeared in her room like . . . Pru couldn't ignore the word that came to mind. It had appeared in her room like *magic*.

Of course, it suddenly struck Pru that it *was* possible her mother had put the card in her room. Pru hadn't considered (or hadn't wanted to consider) that possibility at first because she had wanted to think that the card was special. Now, after everything else that had happened, she wasn't sure what she wanted to think.

"Mom?" she called, and a moment later her mother appeared in the doorway. Pru didn't say anything about the dish towel draped over her mother's shoulder. "Mom, I wanted to show you an envelope I got."

"Pru! Not another letter from school. You said you were going to try harder. You promised there would be no more investigations or wandering off. You promised me!" Her mother paused to put her hand over her face for a moment, stretching her forefinger and thumb to massage each of her temples. She took a deep breath.

"No, it's not like that!" Pru interrupted. She held the envelope in the air between them. "This has nothing to do with stupid school or anything like that. Did you put this in my room?"

Pru's mother blinked.

"Did I put what in your room, sweetie?"

Pru's eyes narrowed as she looked from her mother to the envelope and back again. "This!" she said, waving the envelope in the air. Pru frowned at the vacant expression on her mother's face. Her eyes had strayed to a corner of the room. She'd barely looked at the envelope.

"Hmm? Oh yes, that's very nice, honey. Very nice." Her eyes focused on the envelope briefly, then she appeared to lose interest. She turned and headed back to the kitchen and called to Pru, cheerful but distracted, "The important thing is that it's not another note from school. I know Mrs. Edleman isn't your favorite teacher, but you're stuck with her for the year, so you'd best make the most of it, kiddo."

Pru stared after her mother as she left. She didn't think her mother was lying to her about not knowing about the envelope. It wasn't that Pru didn't think her mother was capable of lying—she knew better than that. But her mother had seemed baffled by the envelope.

No. That wasn't right.

Her mother had seemed baffled but not by the envelope. She hadn't even wanted to look at that. As Pru returned the ever-more-mysterious envelope and its contents to her bag, she found herself thinking once more about who might have sent it—and what it had to do with everything that was happening in Middleton.

✧

Pru spent detention on Tuesday reading about Odin and the other Norse gods. She read that Odin was the god of both wisdom and war, and that brave Viking warriors believed they would go to Odin's hall of Valhalla when they died, while cowards went to the cold, cruel realm of Niflheim, where despair and living corpses dwelt.

It occurred to Pru that Niflheim sounded a lot like detention with Mrs. Edleman.

Mrs. Edleman did not appear to know what to think about Pru reading about Norse myths during detention. This uncharacteristic focus on academic achievement clearly made Mrs. Edleman nervous. Pru frequently caught her teacher stealing glances at her as though trying to catch her doing something wrong. Each time their eyes met, Pru would adopt an innocent expression and Mrs. Edleman would look more worried.

When her time was up, Pru made her way to the abandoned church on Main Street that served as the headquarters of the Earth Center. Inside, volunteers worked in groups to sort the trash they'd gathered into piles appropriate for recycling. Fay stood by the entrance.

"Pru, I was hoping to catch you for just a moment."

"Sure," Pru said as she stifled a groan. She followed Fay into a small office.

"I've already spoken to ABE," Fay said, closing the door behind Pru. "I just wanted to catch you, too, before you head out for the day. I don't usually consider myself an enforcer of rules, but I couldn't help but notice that you and ABE returned without any recyclables after your outing yesterday."

Pru grimaced. In all her excitement over encountering Old Man Grimnir the day before, she had completely forgotten the project.

"Yeah, sorry about that. I was sort of distracted, I guess," Pru said.

"Oh? Is everything all right? Is there something you'd like to talk about?" Fay's voice immediately took on those high, concerned tones that Pru had learned to identify with school counselors, parents, and other adults who wanted to sound caring and supportive.

"I'm fine," she said. "You sound just like my mom."

"Ah, I see. Trouble at home?"

"No," Pru said. Then she remembered the weirdness of her conversation with her mother the night before. She also remembered the tension when her mother had thought she had another note from school. "Maybe. I don't know."

"Have you tried talking to your mom?"

"No."

"Well, I don't want to overstep. I know it's none of my business, really. But do think about talking to your mother about whatever is troubling you, would you? It's usually not a good idea to keep things from the people you love. Secrets build walls between people. And if there's one thing I understand, it's the importance of not building walls." Fay put a hand on Pru's shoulder.

Pru glanced up, surprised by the sincerity in the woman's voice.

"I'll tell you what," Fay said. "We'll overlook yesterday, okay? Just be sure to collect as much as you can today. People are so quick to discard things, even when they still have value."

"Sure," Pru said, eager to leave. "Um . . . are we all done?"

"We are. Happy hunting!" she called as Pru fled out the door.

CHAPTER 11

WITH ABE IN TOW, PRU EXITED THE EARTH CENTER and made her way to Main Street. The road was oddly quiet for the time of day. Plenty of people made their way along the street, passing various shops and businesses, but nearly everyone walked with shoulders hunched and eyes downcast. Nobody looked at the sky, which remained as dark and foreboding as it had for days. Thunder boomed, and half a dozen people around Pru flinched.

"I guess we should get going," Pru said to ABE. They'd agreed that if they were going to make sense of what was happening in Middleton, they would have to try to find Mister Fox. "I wonder where we should start looking."

"Um. Maybe across the street?" ABE said, pointing.

"Very funny, ABE."

"No, Pru, seriously. Look."

Pru turned to see a familiar figure making his way along the other side of Main Street. She couldn't quite believe their luck, but there was no mistaking the identity of the man ABE had spotted. Tall as he was, Mister Fox towered above the hunching residents of Middleton.

"What do you think he's doing here?" ABE asked.

"I don't know. Let's catch up to him and ask." Honestly, she didn't much care what Mister Fox was doing there. The idea of returning to the woods to find him had filled her with dread.

ABE held back. "Wait. Something's weird."

"He's getting too far ahead of us." Pru couldn't believe how quickly he was moving. It was those long legs! Sometimes, being a bit small for your age just seemed an all-around raw deal.

"But look at him. I mean, really watch him for a second."

Pru was inclined to argue, simply out of habit (and to stay in practice), but so many weird things had happened lately that she decided to give ABE the benefit of the doubt.

She watched as Mister Fox approached a small

cluster of people. A series of things happened at the same time. A little boy in a blue windbreaker pulled away from his mother to look in the window of a toy store. The mother followed. A middle-aged man with thinning hair veered suddenly to purchase a newspaper from a dispenser. A woman power walking just behind him moved to the edge of the sidewalk to untie and then retie her shoe.

The same kind of behavior repeated itself in one form or another as Mister Fox continued down the street. To Pru, it looked like Mister Fox projected an invisible shield that deflected people around him.

"Nobody even looks at him," ABE said. "They avoid him, but it's almost like they don't even see him."

The response of the people on the street reminded Pru of her mother's response to the envelope. Pru had held the envelope right in front of her mother, and it had been like she hadn't seen it.

"Look," ABE said, pointing, "he's turning."

Mister Fox turned down Seaside Way. Pru knew the road. It led through a quiet neighborhood of houses laid out in a grid, with trimmed lawns and neat flower-beds. The neighborhood surrendered to the woods that surrounded the town after a bit, but the road continued another quarter of a mile.

"Come on, ABE. If we hurry, we can still catch him

before he gets too far. We can figure out the weird stuff later. We'll add it to the list." Mister Fox was already out of sight. If they didn't hurry, they could lose him.

Pru's sense of urgency made each moment of waiting for a chance to cross Main Street seem like an eternity. When they did cross and turn onto Seaside Way, Pru's fears were realized. Mister Fox wasn't immediately visible.

"Do you think he turned onto one of these side streets?" ABE asked.

"Maybe. You look that way, I'll look on this side."

They reached the end of the stretch of houses without spying Mister Fox.

"Could he have gone into one of the houses? Or do you think he kept going on the road?" ABE asked.

"I don't know." The road was curvy enough that it was possible Mister Fox was just ahead of them, around a bend. "There's not much down there. Just a park with an old fort."

According to Pru's dad, the fort dated back to Revolutionary times. It had an official name, but everyone called it the Fort of the Fallen. It got the nickname from one particularly bloody battle with the British in which nearly everyone—attacker and defender—had died. The town's historical commission preserved the fort because they considered it "a valuable reminder of the vitally important role that history plays in the lives of everyone."

Mostly, teenagers used the parking lot as a spot to make out.

Pru wasn't crazy about leaving behind the comfortable neighborhood and traveling the stretch of road that went through the trees. But it was a short distance, and she figured it would be worth it if they could catch up to Mister Fox and get some questions answered. There was usually a handful of people at the park, anyway, so it wasn't like they were venturing off to the unknown.

That's what Pru kept telling herself as she led ABE down the road. After a few minutes of speed walking (with occasional nervous glances into the woods on either side of the road), they finally reached the Fort of the Fallen where it lay in a cleared section of land along the coast, just east of town and south of Winterhaven House.

The fort's original buildings had long since crumbled and become mounds of grass. The trenches and tunnels that wound around and through the grassy mounds remained, however, like the pathways of an ant farm laid on its side. Once, that network of paths had protected long-ago soldiers from enemy fire. Now, it served to amuse the fort's guests. Town kids (those too young to understand what all the fuss in the parking lot was about) liked to race along the dug-out paths.

The paths were empty that day, though. There didn't appear to be any visitors at all. Beyond the empty parking lot, the open fields of the fort lay shrouded in a thick fog. Pru could hear the ocean waves crashing in the distance and the occasional call of a gull, but the fog muted the sounds and made Pru feel as though she and ABE and the fort were somehow removed from the rest of the world, isolated and alone.

"This doesn't feel right," ABE said quietly. Or perhaps he spoke at a normal level, and the fog muffled his voice just as it muffled the gulls and the waves.

Pru agreed. The fog reminded her of the day in the woods. It was too thick. A small voice in the back of her mind—the one her mother called her conscience—began to whisper that this was not a good idea. For once, Pru felt inclined to listen. She hadn't expected the fort and park to be empty. Even if Mister Fox was there somewhere, Pru no longer felt a strong urge to find him.

Before she could suggest to ABE that they turn around, however, a sudden wind blew across the lot. It carried the fog with it, a thick, unnatural veil of cloudy vapor that swallowed her and ABE whole. Pru spun around in a panic. She realized her mistake, though, as she quickly became disoriented. Her throat closed slightly in fear when she realized she'd even lost sight of ABE.

"ABE!" she whispered.

"I'm here," he responded, and Pru was sure she heard relief in his voice as he stepped into view. Even standing next to her, however, ABE seemed a bit blurred around the edges. It was as though the fog sought to undo him or make him and the world around Pru less certain.

"Pru, I can't see anything. This isn't normal!"

"I know. Let's just get out of here."

"Do you know the way?"

"No. But come on, anyway."

She grabbed the sleeve of ABE's coat with one hand and stretched her other arm out before her to try to feel her way. They'd only managed a few paces before she heard the sound.

Footsteps.

Big, heavy footsteps.

Just like in the woods.

"Pru . . ." ABE muttered behind her.

"Shh!" Pru moved faster. She still didn't know where she was going, but the footsteps gave her an idea of where she didn't want to be.

Dumb luck saved her from a fall. It occurred to her to look down to see if they were still moving along on the pavement. Pru saw immediately they weren't—they'd somehow made it onto the grass. In fact, Pru realized as she looked down that she was barely a step away from falling into one of the trenches that scarred the fort's fields.

The footfalls were getting closer.

Pru whispered to ABE that they should scramble down into the depression. Once at the bottom, Pru led the way through the trenches. The ground rose above her head on either side. She indeed felt like an ant, and that feeling only intensified in those stretches where the trenches ran beneath the earthen mounds and became actual tunnels of dirt and stone.

The footfalls came closer . . . so close that it seemed that whatever was making the noise had to be standing practically on top of them. Pru crouched, pulling ABE down beside her as they peered up into the fog.

The mist above them swirled, shifted by the movements of something impossibly big. All doubt vanished from Pru's mind when the air cleared. No tree stood before them, masquerading as a monster out of a story. It was a giant.

A real, honest-to-goodness giant.

He stood four times as tall as any man, with a rough face, wild hair, and a beard. His clothes looked like what Pru had seen on people at the Explorers' Fair in years past, except his animal skin pants and tunic looked and smelled real. The giant reeked of stale sweat.

Instinctively, Pru knew that this was the same creature

that had chased her and ABE through the woods—
and now he had caught them.

Almost.

The giant looked down and a wicked sneer spread
across his face.

Grabbing ABE by the sleeve, Pru took off along
the trench.

"Pru . . . did you see?" he stammered.

"Yes, ABE, I saw!" Pru hissed. "Less talking. More
running."

The fog closed above them. Ahead, Pru saw the
vague shape of another of the fort's grassy mounds and
thought to hide in the tunnel beneath. But before they
could reach the tunnel's questionable safety, the giant
stumbled into view once more. His foot came down on
the top of the grassy mound above the tunnel's opening and filled the hollow with dirt and debris.

"This way!" ABE said from behind her, and he
took the lead as they dashed back through the trench
in the direction from which they'd come. "Pru, what
are we going to do?"

"Keep moving," she whispered, "and be quiet!" She
remembered how the fog had muffled the sounds of the
waves and the birds when they first arrived at the fort.
Maybe she and ABE could make that work for them.

Though the fog once more offered some cover, Pru
still caught occasional glimpses of the giant when she

looked over her shoulder. Those glances told her that the creature was moving slowly, as though unsure of what direction to go. The trenches through which she and ABE ran branched so often, and the fog was so thick, the giant had lost them.

ABE must have understood Pru's caution, because he slowed a bit and began moving more quietly. He led them a little farther along the winding trail. When they reached a spot where an outcropping of earth mostly covered their path, Pru put a hand on ABE's shoulder and stopped him. They settled into another crouch.

The giant moved nearby, but his movements sounded slow and uncertain. Another breeze shifted the fog overhead and Pru saw to her horror that the giant had stopped just above them with one foot on either side of the trench in which she hid with ABE.

The giant peered into the fog ahead. Pru held her breath and prayed that he would not look directly down.

After what seemed like forever, the giant began to move away, disappearing into the mist. Pru was just about to sigh with relief when a hand, too big to be ABE's, reached out from behind her and rested on her shoulder.

Acting on instinct, she put her elbows to good use.

With a muffled grunt, the figure behind her let go—and Pru spun around to find Mister Fox standing there with one hand rubbing his rib cage.

"You're a very violent little girl," he whispered. "Has anyone ever told you that?"

"Yes! And don't call me little," Pru hissed back, wondering what, exactly, a heart attack felt like and whether eleven-year-olds could get them.

"Mister Fox?" ABE looked as surprised as Pru to find him there. "You're not going to believe this, but there's a giant out there. Honest. It's a real, live giant."

"I know. Beautiful, isn't it?" Mister Fox peered into the mist. His nose was twitching.

"You mean it's good?" Pru asked.

"Good? That's a Jotun—a frost giant. They're extremely warlike. No, we're in terrible danger," Mister Fox said, sounding alarmingly cheerful. "Now shush, please, I need to take care of this. Fantastic a specimen as our large friend is, I can't just leave him wandering about. Someone's likely to get hurt."

"Someone?" ABE squeaked.

"What are you going to do?" Pru asked.

"I'm going to use this," Mister Fox said, reaching into the inner pocket of his coat. She was relieved (if a little confused) when he pulled out the magnifying glass she had seen him use before.

"You're going to use a magnifying glass? On a giant?" ABE's eyes went from Mister Fox to where they'd last seen the giant. "Sorry, *but isn't he big enough already?*"

"If it's any comfort to you, it's only a magnifying

95

glass if you look through it in one direction," Mister Fox explained. He was enjoying himself way too much, as far as Pru was concerned. "Look into the glass from the other direction and the surface is reflective, like a mirror. Which makes it, I think you'll agree, the very epitome of a looking glass."

"What difference does that make?" Pru asked.

"Quite a bit of difference, I think. You'd be surprised by how many of life's little problems can be solved by taking either a closer look at the problem—or a closer look at yourself."

"Little problems?" ABE echoed. He sounded like he'd swallowed enough helium to float a thousand balloons.

"Here's what I need you two to do." Mister Fox spoke over ABE. "When I give the signal, run along the trench in that direction. There's a mound just ahead. Run until you get to the tunnel beneath the mound, then hide inside." Without further explanation, Mister Fox took two steps back and disappeared into the fog.

"Wait! What's the signal?" Pru whispered. There was no response.

A moment later, an earsplitting whistle broke the muffled silence.

"Um, I think that was the signal," ABE said, and they took off running.

The mound appeared ahead, just as Mister Fox had described. To her horror, though, Pru saw that an iron gate barred the entrance to the tunnel. A sign on the gate read DEAD END, which Pru might have found amusing if she had been watching this happen to someone else in a movie.

"Now what?" ABE asked as Pru grabbed the bars with both fists and shook them to no avail.

Before she could answer, the giant bounded into view, homing in on the sound of the rattling bars and sweeping away the fog with his quick movements.

The creature raised one arm above his head and curled his fingers together with terrible purpose. With the fog gone, Pru could watch each finger settle into place. She imagined she could hear the leathery skin stretching over the knuckles and each muscle tightening as the enormous fist formed.

Another whistle screamed through the air, and Pru looked up to the top of the earthen mound behind them. Mister Fox stood above, flourishing his long coat to clear the mist that swirled around him. His outstretched arm held his magnifying glass.

The giant also looked toward the source of the whistling sound. The instant the giant looked at the glass, there was a flash of golden light so bright that Pru had to cover her eyes.

When she opened them, the giant had vanished.

CHAPTER 12

THE AIR WHERE THE GIANT HAD STOOD SHIMMERED for a moment. Then the effect vanished and the Fort of the Fallen grew still.

"What just happened?" Pru asked Mister Fox. "Where did the giant go? Did you kill him?"

Mister Fox sniffed and the twitching of his nose subsided. "Kill him? Hardly my style. I simply sent him back to where he came from."

"How?" ABE asked.

"With this, of course." Mister Fox held out his looking glass. The glass itself was ringed by brass, which gave way to a wooden handle, blackened in spots with age. More brass had been fashioned into the shape of a fox's head at the base of the handle. It reminded Pru of the pommel of a sword.

"How did that get rid of the giant?" ABE asked.

"Never mind that, ABE," Pru interrupted. "How was there a giant in the first place? Giants aren't real. *How was there a giant?*"

"You have questions," Mister Fox said, slipping the fox-head looking glass into the inner pocket of his coat. "That's understandable. It's good, even."

"So you'll answer them?" ABE asked.

"Oh no. But I'll tell you what I will do," Mister Fox said with a final twitch of his nose. "I'll tell you a story."

"We don't need stories!" Pru said. "We need answers. *That was a giant.*"

"On the contrary, answers are the last thing you need right now. Answers stop you from thinking, and you're no good to me at all if that happens. A story is exactly what you need. A story will get you thinking." Mister Fox looked around. "Not here, though. There could be other dangers lurking about."

Before Pru could ask what other dangers he was talking about, Mister Fox set off. Pru hesitated, noticing that ABE seemed equally uncertain what to do.

"You can stay if you want," Mister Fox called back as if he'd read their minds. "But your town is in danger, and you two are in the unique position to be of some help. Possibly. But only if you're bold enough."

"Pru, I'm not sure we should . . ."

"What choice do we have, ABE? We just saw a giant. A for-real giant. Impossible things are happening. And he's the only one who seems to know anything about it. And if the town really is in danger . . ." She shook her head and hugged her arms to her chest. "Besides, do we really want to stay here by ourselves?"

ABE's eyes widened at that, and they set off to follow Mister Fox.

"A good story," he was saying as they fell into step beside him. "*That* will sort you out. A good story will get you asking questions and get you thinking. That's how you'll make sense of what just happened."

"I don't think what just happened will ever make sense," ABE said, glancing back over his shoulder.

"We'll see," Mister Fox said. "This happens to be a very good story. One of my favorites, in fact. And it starts like this—once upon a time, there lived a peaceful witch who was terrorized by a wicked village."

"Uh, sorry," ABE said when Mister Fox paused for a breath, "but did you maybe say that part backward?"

"If you're going to tell us a story, at least tell it right," Pru insisted.

"I'm telling it just fine, thank you. Or I would be, if you two weren't so quick to interrupt me."

"Sorry," ABE said.

"I'd still rather have answers," Pru muttered. The exit from the park to which Mister Fox was leading them would take them back into the woods. Somehow, Pru wasn't surprised when she realized that if they kept going straight, they'd arrive at the cemetery.

"As I was saying," Mister Fox continued, "once upon a time there was a peaceful witch who was terrorized by a wicked village. Mind you, the village didn't start out wicked. When the village first rose up in the ancient forests of what we now call Russia, the villagers were thrilled to discover they had a witch for a sometimes neighbor."

"What do you mean, 'a sometimes neighbor'?" Pru asked.

"The witch traveled a lot. She had a magical house that could go anywhere. Think of it as the first mobile home, only made entirely of wood and—well, other parts. Anyway, the witch traveled all over in her magical house. But since even houses have their homes, the witch returned regularly to the spot near the village in the Russian forest. When she did return, the people of the village flocked to the witch to ask her about her journeys. And the witch answered their questions, every last one, despite the cost to her."

"What kind of cost?" Pru asked. "Why should she have to pay for answering their questions?"

"She shouldn't have had to. But witches are magical beings, and when it comes to magic, there's always a cost involved. So it was with the witch. In her case, it happened that every time she answered a question she aged one year."

"What? Seriously?" Pru shook her head. "If I was the witch, I would have sent those people packing. Or turned them into toads, maybe. Or newts." Pru was not exactly sure what a newt was, but she was under the general impression they were the sort of thing associated with witches.

"Well," Mister Fox replied, "then I suppose it's lucky for those villagers that you weren't there. The witch was more generous. Witches are long-lived, you see, so at first the loss of a few years didn't matter to her. And, more importantly, the witch loved sharing her stories about distant lands. She loved the villagers' curiosity and was glad to encourage it. But things changed, over time, as they always do."

"What do you mean? What changed?" ABE asked.

"Everything. The witch, the village, the world. Ages of enchantment gave way to ages of reason and industry. As humankind grew up, humans lost their fascination with witches and the wider world. I guess you could say that the bigger the world got, the smaller the minds of people in the village grew. As the village became a town, the townspeople cared less for stories of faraway places and became far more focused on themselves and their own well-being. They became distrustful of things that were different, especially witches. Of course, that didn't stop them from visiting the witch still, on occasion."

"Why would they visit her if they didn't trust her?" ABE asked.

"You'd be amazed what most people can overlook when it benefits them to do so. The witch had a lot to offer. She was an excellent healer. The best. And she still knew many answers the people sought. If they wanted to know about a particular ailment or injury, or why their crops weren't growing, or if they had troubles with a neighbor, they would visit the witch. They continued to borrow knowledge against the witch's years. They stole her youth and, in time, they stole her middle years, too."

"But why did the witch let them?" Pru protested. "Why didn't she stop them somehow, or just leave? That's what I would have done. Or the toad thing." She'd given up on newts. The whole idea of newts seemed too vague.

"Eventually, the witch did leave. But it took time. She kept hoping, I think, that things would go back to the way they'd been and that the townspeople would rediscover their curiosity and their tolerance. They didn't. They did give the witch something in return, though, before she left the forest. They gave her a new name to replace the forgotten name of the young woman the witch had been, back at the start. They named her Baba Yaga. Sometime after that, the witch Baba Yaga took her house and she left the forests of Russia."

"Where did she go?" ABE asked.

"Here and there," Mister Fox said, shrugging. "Also hither and yon, probably. She traveled about while she could. It wasn't as easy as it had once been, though. She'd lost so many years. And still, from time to time, people would approach her with questions. In time, Baba Yaga took measures to frighten such people off and protect her remaining years. She encouraged the rumors that were spreading about her, rumors that said she ate children and such. It worked, too, more or less."

As Mister Fox spoke and the trio walked on, the area through which they traveled began to look familiar to Pru. Their trail must have intersected with the trail she and ABE had taken the last time they'd ventured into the woods. Pru shivered, remembering.

"Are you sure this is safe?" she asked.

"There aren't any giants here," Mister Fox replied before continuing with his story. "Now, for the most part, people learned to avoid the house of Baba Yaga. There were exceptions, of course. I know of at least one person who approached the witch's house, despite the rumors."

"Who?" ABE asked.

"A young boy, about your age. He'd heard the stories of the terrible Baba Yaga. So when he came upon her house, there was a part of him that wanted to run. Part of him wanted to flee to someplace safe and familiar. He didn't, though."

"Why not?" ABE asked. Pru could tell from ABE's tone that fleeing seemed like the sensible option to him.

"Well, as far as feeling safe goes, it's possible that the boy felt like there was no place he could return to that *was* safe. He was lost, in so many ways. And the thing about familiar places is that they *are* so familiar. There's nothing new there, nothing to discover. And though he was lost and frightened, somewhere deep within him the boy still had a love for exploration. So, in the end, you could say that the boy did not run away because he was curious. And I think Baba Yaga sensed that genuine curiosity, because she eventually accepted the boy into her home."

Still some ways ahead, the small shed that Pru had glimpsed the last time she and ABE had been in the woods came into view. They had reached the border of the cemetery.

"Inside the house of Baba Yaga, the boy encountered

things both terrifying and wondrous. And, naturally, the witch had him for dinner."

ABE paled.

"By which I mean she *invited* him to dinner," Mister Fox continued. "Much to the boy's relief, Baba Yaga did not eat the boy right away. She threatened to. She had a reputation to maintain, after all. But she fed him and gave him a place to sleep. Then she set him some chores around her house. They were difficult. Since Baba Yaga's house is a fantastic and impossible place, household chores take on a whole new meaning. But the witch told the boy that if he finished the chores and did not ask any questions, she would let him live. And that's just what the boy did. Oh, he had plenty of questions. But he set about finding his own answers."

As they drew closer to the shack, Pru noticed with some surprise a thin tendril of smoke snaking its way from a small chimney. She wouldn't have thought the shack or shed or whatever it was would be large enough to have a fireplace.

"Weeks passed like that, then months. Every day, the witch set the boy a new task and every night she'd say, 'Well done, my little Mister Fox.' That was a name she'd taken to calling him. 'You've a clever mind and you answer your own questions. I think I'll let you live another day. But I'll probably have you for breakfast tomorrow.'"

At the mention of the boy's name, Pru and ABE exchanged startled looks.

"She never did have the boy for breakfast, though. Because in him Baba Yaga found something she'd long searched for—someone like her. She'd found someone curious enough to ask questions but clever enough to seek his own answers. Baba Yaga and the boy lived together for a time like mother and son. After a while, she built the boy a house, much like her own.

"Baba Yaga explained to the boy that there were whole other worlds beyond ours out there, connected to us by avenues of possibility and perception—worlds of magic, where witches live, and giants, and so much more. The boy's new house would take him to those places. It would take him anywhere imaginable.

"And after she had explained to the boy about the wonders of his new house, she set him his one final task. He was to travel in his magical home and explore those worlds. He was to ask questions and seek answers. He was to discover and investigate all the mysteries of magic and rejoice in them. And, finally, he was to return to the witch from time to time and share what he had learned. Because Baba Yaga had given those villagers and her young Mister Fox almost all her years, and travel for her was hard."

Mister Fox moved more quickly now, and soon they were standing before the old shack.

"It was much less than the witch deserved as payment for all the kindness and generosity she'd shown over the years, but it was the best the boy could do. So that's exactly what he agreed to do, for as long as he could."

Stopping, Mister Fox turned to look at Pru and ABE.

"Well, then, here we are."

"What do you mean?" Pru asked. "Where's here?"

"My home," Mister Fox said, and he gestured grandly to the miserable little shack behind him. "Welcome to the Henhouse."

CHAPTER 13

"YOU LIVE IN *THAT*?" PRU ASKED.

"You call your house the Henhouse?" ABE said at the same time.

"Yes. On both counts." Mister Fox turned to ABE and tipped his hat. His chest was puffed out in pride. "I call it the Henhouse for two reasons. First, I like the sound of it. Come on. Fox in a Henhouse? That's fantastic. Admit it."

"What's the other reason?" ABE asked, admitting nothing.

Mister Fox didn't answer, but his nose twitched.

"No," Pru said. "Seriously. You *live* in that?" The shack looked like a once-grand house that had been shrunk down to the size of a garden shed and then left to the rain and rot for a few dozen years. A rusted weather vane in the shape of a hen rose up from the roof. It squeaked slightly as it turned to face her.

There wasn't any wind.

She began to walk about the ramshackle hut, noticing with distaste the rotted wood and boarded windows. As she completed her loop, she saw something that assured her that Mister Fox was joking.

"You can't live here. This thing doesn't even have a door."

"Doesn't it?" Mister Fox asked with exaggerated surprise.

Pru's certainty faltered as he retraced her path and disappeared around one corner. Had she missed something?

"Why, you seem to be right," Mister Fox said as he circled around the Henhouse and appeared on the other side. He walked between and past Pru and ABE. They both turned their back to the shack to follow him with their eyes. Mister Fox faced them again, his coat sweeping the autumn leaves around his ankles, and ducked his chin and adjusted the brim of his hat, pulling it low over his face. The action blocked Pru's view of his eyes and his nose, big as it was. The hat didn't quite cover his mouth, though, not from where Pru stood. Sometimes it helped, being small for one's age. She carefully watched his lips move and saw that he was muttering some sort of incantation.

As Pru studied Mister Fox's lips, she heard a sound like the rustling of feathers. She turned to look back at the Henhouse.

An ornate, arched set of double doors now occupied the side facing her. They stood atop a rickety porch. A round window stood directly above the doors, like a single, unblinking eye. The window was decorated with a complicated pattern of interlocking circles.

"Where did those doors come from?" ABE asked, staring.

"I think you'll find that the Henhouse is full of surprises." Mister Fox approached the double doors. Pru heard a click as he turned the knobs and the latches in the doors released. Curiously, she also heard a string of identical clicks, each sounding a moment after the one before it, like a dozen other doors being opened one after another.

"It's funny . . . we were talking about Baba Yaga just now. There are so many stories about her, but here's the thing. They never get the house right. Some of the stories say that Baba Yaga's house was so small that she had to curl up to fit inside and that her knees and nose scraped the ceiling. Other stories describe a house filled with rooms and servants. And in all this time, no one's tried to reconcile those two images."

With that, Mister Fox pushed open the double doors. He had to stoop to do so, as the top of the arched door-frame barely reached the top of his head. Pru expected the doors to open to a ratty little room occupied by spiders or bats or other assorted vermin.

They didn't.

Instead, the doors opened to reveal another set of double doors exactly like the first, only slightly larger. They, in turn, opened on their own, revealing yet *another* set of doors. This continued until, in just moments, a long, arched hallway stretched out in front of Mister Fox, expanding in size as it went.

"But that's not possible," ABE said. Eyes wide, he sidestepped to the edge of the building and peered around the corner. Pru knew that he was discovering what she already knew from circling the Henhouse earlier.

"It doesn't fit," she said. "That hallway . . . it's longer than the whole house."

"It's impossible," ABE insisted, returning to stand next to Pru.

"How?" Pru asked. Her voice sounded faraway to her own ears, like a part of her was already racing down that impossible hallway to discover the wonders inside.

"No." The curt word cut through the air and snapped Pru back to herself. "That's the wrong question." Mister Fox's voice was solemn. And though the laughter still lurked in the depths of his eyes, they shone with challenge.

"What do you mean?" Pru asked.

"If you two learned anything from the story I told you, you should at least have learned that answers aren't just valuable. Sometimes, they're expensive. Now, I'm not a witch. I'm not going to age with every answer I give. But that doesn't mean I give them out freely. Answers have to be earned. Sometimes, that can be done by asking the right question. Pru and ABE, the answers to everything that's happened to you, that's happening to your town . . . and to so much more . . . all those answers wait inside this house. But you don't get to learn them, not unless you ask the right question."

To anyone else, Mister Fox's challenge might have seemed daunting. But Pru knew what question to ask. She'd been carrying it around in her messenger bag for days. She'd been seeing the words of the question in her mind's eye for just as long, golden words on a field of inky blue.

"WHAT IS THE 'UNBELIEVABLE FIB'?" she quoted, and a thrill ran up her spine as she spoke the words aloud and, for the first time, felt hope for an answer.

Mister Fox relaxed and his grin settled on his face with the ease of a frequent guest.

"Now *that* is a good question. And do you know what good questions are? They're invitations. Good questions are like invitations to learn something new. You may come inside," he said, and his voice carried an unusual formality when he spoke the words. "Or you may go home. But this is an invitation you'll only receive once."

With that, Mister Fox turned to enter the Henhouse. He paused just long enough to add, "Mind the toes." Then he continued on. He had to duck as he passed beneath the first couple of archways. After that, the hallway through which he walked opened and expanded around him, and he stood at his full height.

"Pru," ABE said, and there was caution in his voice.

Pru understood. For all the mystery and magic of the moment, following Mister Fox into his impossible house still amounted to entering a stranger's home, something that all children learn at a young age never to do.

"He saved our lives." Pru wasn't sure whether she said it to reassure ABE or herself.

ABE opened his mouth to respond but closed it a moment later, looking thoughtful.

Pru still didn't cross the threshold. Instead, she called after Mister Fox. "You said our town was in danger. Is it still, with the giant gone? And if it *is* still in danger, will following you help?"

"Perhaps," Mister Fox called back. He didn't turn or pause.

"Perhaps? 'Perhaps' to what? To the danger, or to it helping?"

But Mister Fox had vanished into the Henhouse, and no other answer was forthcoming.

Pru looked at ABE, who sighed. Then she stepped into the Henhouse. The wood of the floor felt surprisingly soft beneath her feet, and the air smelled of green and growing things. Pru moved in farther and ABE stepped up behind her. Together they walked down the impossible hallway. Ribbed as it was with doorframes every few feet, it reminded Pru of the gullet of some giant beast. Even though the space around them grew with every step, Pru couldn't quite escape the feeling that they were being swallowed whole.

She quickened her step, and before too long the arched hallway opened into a space so large that Pru could only stare, openmouthed, as she stepped into it and caught up to Mister Fox.

The room at the end of the arched hallway stretched out in every direction, larger than three of Middleton Elementary School's gymnasiums put together. Doors lined the walls. Each door stood between two columns. Each column was carved to look like a tree trunk, complete with a complicated network of branches that reached out and laced together with the branches of its neighbor on either side to form an entangled arch over every door.

The forest of columns supported a second story to the building, where that same pattern was repeated: more doors, more columns, and another story above. Each floor stood slightly set back from the one below it, so that walkways circled the open space in the center of the room. Pru tried to count the number of floors rising above and expanding around her, but her head began to spin and she lost count.

Oil lamps hung from the treelike columns and filled the space with a warm, golden glow, like a forest glade in the first moments of an autumn sunset. Shadows grew from where the light hit the doorframe branches. Those shadows stretched across walls and ceilings. They shifted and swayed with each flicker of light, like actual tree limbs caught in a gentle breeze. It was as though the inside of the Henhouse were the extension of an actual forest, ancient and grand. Any anxiety Pru had felt about entering the Henhouse slipped away as she stood in the gentle glow of Mister Fox's magnificent home.

"Names first, before we go any further. Names are important," Mister Fox said, partially breaking the spell. He turned to ABE first, who was closest. "You are?"

"Oh." With an apparent effort, ABE turned his

attention away from the spectacle before them and focused on the question. "Um, I'm ABE."

"No. You're not."

Mister Fox spoke with hardly a hesitation. When ABE blinked his confusion, Mister Fox explained, "You paused before you answered. That's usually an indication that someone's not telling the truth. Trust me, I know about such things."

"Oh. That. Well, A-B-E is sort of a nickname. They're my initials."

"Are they? Well, then, that's different. I like people who go by their initials. They're the sort of people who stand for something. And you?" He turned to Pru.

For just a moment, Prudence Potts considered introducing herself by her initials. She quickly thought better of it.

"I'm Pru. Well, Prudence, really, but I prefer *Pru*. How is this possible?" she blurted before Mister Fox could say anything else.

"Walk with me while I explain. Stay close. The Henhouse can play tricks with a person's sense of space and direction." He set off, heading toward a staircase Pru hadn't noticed before. "Have you ever heard of Russian nesting dolls?"

ABE spoke up when Pru didn't answer. "Aren't they those hollow wooden dolls that fit inside each other? One wooden figure is placed inside another one that looks just like it, only bigger, and so on."

"Exactly right." Mister Fox nodded and spun about once, his arms extended to gesture to the space around them. "Think of the Henhouse as being like that. Imagine it's a series of houses all occupying the same space, but each one is a little larger than the one inside it. The only difference is that, in this case, it's like someone reached in and turned the whole thing inside out, so that the smallest house is on the outside and each copy gets progressively larger as you move inward."

"But that's not possible," Pru said.

"I think you'll find that what is possible and what is not possible is a far less certain thing than most people imagine. The point is, can you picture what I'm describing?"

"I suppose so," Pru admitted.

"There you go. That's what magic is. Magic is something that seems absolutely impossible until you think about it in just the right way. Then it makes perfect sense."

Mister Fox continued to lead the way through the Henhouse. As they ascended to a new level, Pru slowed her steps and peered over the railing. A wave of vertigo washed over her.

They'd climbed so high! She couldn't remember

climbing that many stairs, but the main floor lay far enough below that she could barely make out the details of the doors through which they'd entered.

"Pru!"

She looked up as ABE spoke her name, shocked to see that he and Mister Fox had already turned the corner and were nearing another set of stairs a good distance away. Pru had to run to catch them.

When they had first entered the Henhouse, it appeared to Pru that some of the many doors visible around the grand inner courtyard were open. And yet every door they passed stood closed. Now and again, Pru thought she heard sounds from behind the doors.

"Do other people live here?" she asked.

"People? No. Not as such. Just me and the *domovye*."

"*Domovye?*"

"Russian household spirits."

"Your house is haunted?" ABE asked, stumbling as he tried to look in every direction around them at once.

"It's a house that typically resides in a cemetery and was built by a witch. Are you really surprised? But don't worry. The *domovye* are mostly harmless, if at times a bit mischievous. They can actually even be helpful and protective, so long as you don't upset them. Most houses just have one, if any. The Henhouse is something of a special case."

Mister Fox led them up a crooked stairway all the

119

way to the uppermost level of the Henhouse, to what Pru would have considered the attic in any other home. There, in the canopy that grew from the forest of columns below, carved branches reached up through the floor and climbed to the top of the vaulted ceiling above. Lanterns hung throughout the twisting labyrinth of tree limbs and painted more shadows on roof and wall.

Pru and ABE followed their host through that enchanted woodland with its glowing, fairy-light lanterns toward a round window that hung like a moon on the far end of the room. It reached from the floor to the ceiling and was adorned with a wood frame made up of a pattern of interlocked circles. It looked identical to the window Pru had seen above the front door of the Henhouse, only much, much larger.

Mister Fox turned to face his guests as he reached the window. Beyond him, through the glass, sprawled the whole of Middleton Cemetery as seen from a great height. Pru struggled to reconcile how high they were from the ground with her memory of the tiny shack.

"What I'm about to tell you isn't a secret," Mister Fox began. "It's a truth. There's a difference, of course. Secrets are the things that we keep from other people. Truths? Truths are the things we keep from ourselves. And there's one truth people have been keeping from themselves for a very long time now."

CHAPTER

14

A SHIVER RAN THROUGH PRU. AT FIRST, SHE THOUGHT it was just a response to Mister Fox's words, something that bubbled up from inside her like the feeling she got on Christmas morning when she climbed from her bed and wondered what waited in the living room, beneath the tree.

But there was more to it than that. The whole room seemed to shiver. The glass in the window rippled like someone had tossed a handful of pebbles into a pool of water. The ripples repeated the pattern of interlocked circles. Each outer circle intersected the center ring at a different point. It looked a bit like a child's drawing of a flower. The ripples moved beyond the glass. Pru saw waves pass through the air. She felt them, too, like a gentle breeze on her skin.

The breeze gained intensity as it moved past Pru and pushed into the room behind her. It extinguished every lantern in quick succession, like candles on a birthday cake, until the room went utterly black. The window went black, too, and the world beyond disappeared.

Pru tensed as the darkness swallowed her. But in the shocked moment between breaths, before panic could rise, a pinprick of light appeared. Pru followed the point of light with her eyes as it began to move through the air, tracing the pattern that had covered the window: one circle in the center, surrounded by a cluster of others.

The glowing pattern cast just enough light for Pru to see ABE and Mister Fox on either side of her. Beyond that, Pru floated in a void.

"The truth, which you've already begun to discover, is that magic is real," Mister Fox continued. "There are whole worlds of magic out there, all around us."

As he spoke, images began to form in the space before Pru. An image of the earth spun into view from out of the darkness and moved to occupy the center circle in the pattern. More pictures followed. New landscapes appeared, each in a different circle. Each new scene offered a glimpse into a different, fantastic world.

Pru saw a world where long, narrow boats floated

on a river of fire past giant pyramids. She saw another world where a man in a flowing white robe and oiled hair stood high atop a mountain, above a host of pillared temples. He held lightning in his fist as he surveyed his domain. A third circle showed a gathering of women and men in flowing silks of every shade of green, keeping company with serpentine dragons.

"How are you doing this? How are you making those pictures appear?" ABE asked, his voice a whisper in the dark.

"It's called scrying," Mister Fox said. "It's an old magic. Anything that can reflect an image, like glass in a window, can work if you know the right charm or spell. But it's not me making it happen, it's the Henhouse."

"What are these places? What are we looking at?" Pru asked.

"Each place has its own name, of course. You've heard of some of them. The High Hills and five rings of Atlantis, mentioned by the Greeks. The Heavenly Ministry of the Great Emperor of the Eastern Peak, discovered by the ancient Chinese, with its troubled bureaucracy and three fateful bridges. The infernal river that runs through the twelve provinces down to the Hall of Two Truths of Egyptian mythology. The blessed Isle of Avalon, where kings sleep and wizards wait. But there are many more."

The tone of Mister Fox's voice drew Pru's gaze

from the window. Wonder spread across his face, revealed by the glowing and changing light of the magical vision before them. Pru thought she saw something else there, as well. She'd seen the same look on her own face in the mirror in the days after her dad's death. Loss, and longing. Pru wondered if Mister Fox was thinking about Baba Yaga.

"Collectively," Mister Fox continued, "it might be easier for you to think of them as Worlds of Myth, because the beings that live in those realms inspired the stories that we call myths today."

"Mythology is real?" Pru asked, her attention returning to the window. "Myths are true?"

"Yes. And also no, not always. Think of it this way. There's at least a seed of truth in them. But it's the nature of stories to change with each telling, and most myths have been told and retold a great many times."

Each circle in the pattern was filled now, and it seemed to Pru there were more than there had been at the start.

"This is all kind of hard to believe," ABE said in his quiet way.

Mister Fox spun away from the window. As he did, the images vanished and the light slowly faded from the room. Mister Fox's voice floated through the darkness. It reminded Pru of that first day at Winterhaven House.

"Don't believe me."

Someone snapped his fingers (Pru assumed it was Mister Fox), and all the lanterns in the room flared back to life. As they did, the view of the cemetery returned.

"That's the last thing in the world I want you to do," Mister Fox said.

"What?" Pru blinked as her eyes struggled to adjust to the sudden absence of the dark and all the mysteries it had revealed. "Why wouldn't you want us to believe you?"

"Because you're no good to me at all if you believe me. It's like I said to you two before, back in the woods, belief is a powerful thing. Belief changes the whole way a person sees the world. It's because people nowadays believe so easily that they can't see magic, they can't see beings from Worlds of Myth."

"But books and movies are always saying you *have* to believe in magic to see it," Pru argued, armed with a childhood of evidence to support her claim.

"Don't remind me." Mister Fox threw himself into a large chair in the center of the room. Pru was sure the chair hadn't been there when they came in. Had the household spirits—the *domovye*—placed it there while the lights were out? Pru glanced around, hoping in vain to catch a glimpse of one as Mister Fox continued.

"Don't get me wrong. It's a lovely idea. It's very

romantic. 'Just believe' and you can experience magic. It's why grandmothers the world over knit the word *Believe* into blankets for grandchildren." His elbows resting on the arms of his chair, Mister Fox waved his hands in a vague, circular gesture. "There's just one little problem. It's completely wrong. It's backward. When you believe in something, you stop questioning it. You stop looking for answers and ignore other possibilities. Only minds that are truly open to possibility can see magic. It's people who aren't sure—of themselves, of the world, of their place in the world—who can see and experience magic."

"Sorry, excuse me," ABE said, half raising his hand to ask a question. "When you said we'd be 'no good to you' just a minute ago, what, ah, exactly did you mean by that?"

"Of course, it wasn't always like that," Mister Fox said, continuing as though ABE hadn't spoken. "People didn't always believe too easily. Back in the beginning, back when the world was new, people had no idea what to believe. They questioned everything. 'Why does the sun move across the sky?' 'Why does the earth shake?' 'Why does it rain?' They didn't know, so they imagined possibilities. And because they imagined possibilities, their minds opened and they witnessed fantastic things."

"They saw beings from the Worlds of Myth?" Pru asked, beginning to understand.

"Exactly." Mister Fox stretched out his legs and crossed his ankles. "I call them Mythics, because it gets tiresome saying 'beings from Worlds of Myth' over and over again. But, yes. They saw chariots racing across the sky. They saw great serpents whose movements shook the earth itself. They saw beings with god-like powers who could control the very elements of weather. And all those things became the seeds of the myths we know now."

"What happened, then?" ABE asked. "How come people can't see beings . . . ah, *Mythics*, anymore? Well, except us?"

"You know what happened. I told you. The world changed. Humankind marched on and traded wonder for certainty. People stopped asking so many questions and started believing in answers. Oh, there were individual exceptions, of course, but for the most part that was the way of the world."

"Like the villagers changing how they thought about the witch."

"Just like that. But this is what you have to understand. The Worlds of Myth are still out there. And every once upon a while, something from one of those worlds travels here. It doesn't happen often. Mythics have grown comfortable in their realms, too, and this world of technology and certainty doesn't much appeal to them. But every so often, something from a World of Myth comes here. When it does, trouble often follows."

"So that's the answer, then, isn't it?" Pru interrupted. "That's what 'THE UNBELIEVABLE FIB' is. The fib is that magic isn't real, because the truth is it *is real*." Pru raised her chin, a look of triumph on her face.

"Nope." Removing his hat, Mister Fox tossed it so it landed neatly on a nearby branch. Then he clasped his hands behind his head and leaned back. "No, 'THE UNBELIEVABLE FIB' is the name of my detective agency."

"*What?*" Pru asked.

"FIB stands for Fantasy Investigation Bureau. That's what I do. I investigate the mysteries that arise when something fantastic from a World of Myth enters this world. I did tell you that I liked people who went by their initials. Honestly, you two *have* to start paying attention."

"So you *are* a detective!" Pru exclaimed.

"I am."

"But that doesn't make sense," ABE interrupted.

"You don't think a person who investigates mythology can be called a detective?" Mister Fox asked. "What are myths, except people's earliest attempts to solve the mysteries of the world around them? That's what detectives do, right? They solve mysteries. If you ask me, detectives and mythology go hand in hand."

"No," ABE said, shaking his head in an apparent effort to get the right words out. "Well, yes, I see what you mean about that. But what you said before isn't right. I mean, the name of your detective agency doesn't make sense. I get that you investigate fantastic things, but a 'bureau' isn't just one person. It's a group of people, isn't it?"

"Ah, that." The detective nodded. "You're right about that, of course. But you're assuming I work alone. I don't. Remember, the Henhouse is special. It was built by a witch and it's drawn to magic. So when a Mythic enters this world from a World of Myth, the Henhouse takes me to wherever the crossing takes place.

"As soon as I arrive, I recruit some locals to help me out. Unfortunately, as we've discussed, very few people can see magic, nowadays. So I send the *domovye* out to deliver invitations with a question and a clue. Since the invitations come from the Henhouse, they're magical themselves and can only be seen by the right sort of people. Anyone else has a hard time focusing their vision and their thoughts on them. Magic exists outside their worldview, so to speak, so they get easily distracted."

"So me and ABE are the right sort of people?"

"It would appear so."

"About that," ABE said, looking away. "I didn't actually get an invitation, exactly."

"What?" For the first time since Pru had met him, Mister Fox looked surprised. He leapt from his chair and, crouching to eye level, studied ABE intently, as though trying to see through a disguise. "That's not possible. No one can find the Henhouse without an invitation."

"He saw mine," Pru said as something occurred to her. "ABE just moved here. Maybe that's why he didn't get one."

Mister Fox looked from Pru back to ABE, who nodded.

"I didn't get into town until Thursday afternoon. I'm new here . . . It's sort of been an adjustment. My last town didn't have giants."

"That could explain it, I suppose," the detective said, straightening. "The *domovye* wouldn't leave an invitation at a house with nobody in it."

"But you still haven't explained *why* you send the cards," Pru said.

"The Henhouse takes me all over the world to investigate. When I arrive somewhere new, I need to connect with locals who can see Mythics *and* who know their way around. The Henhouse brought me here because Middleton is in danger. I need people who know the town and can help point out anything unusual or out of place."

"You keep saying the town's in danger," ABE said. "Because of the giant? But you got rid of the giant, right? How did you do that, anyway?"

"Tell me," Mister Fox said, removing the fox-head looking glass from his pocket and cradling it in his hand. "Do you know that feeling you get when you're caught being somewhere you don't belong?"

"Yes," Pru said.

"No," ABE said. Then he added, thoughtfully, "Well, I didn't until I met Pru, I guess."

The corner of his mouth twitching, Mister Fox said, "Deep down, Mythics know they don't belong in this world. My looking glass is enchanted. The domovye made it. One of its tricks is the ability to magnify, so to speak, that feeling of not belonging to such a degree that it becomes impossible for any Mythic that sees itself in the mirror to remain here."

"So the giant's gone," Pru said.

"That one is, yes, banished back to where he came from."

"That one?" ABE asked. Pru noticed that his voice had begun to squeak again. "Are there more?"

"That's not the important question," Mister Fox said.

"Sorry, but . . . are you sure?" ABE asked. "It seems kind of important to me."

"The important question is, why was the frost giant here in the first place?"

Pru considered a moment. Why *would* a frost giant come to Middleton?

"I think I know!" she said, surprising herself almost as much as ABE, who flinched at her sudden exclamation. Mister Fox eyed her but remained silent. Pru spoke slowly, choosing each word with care. "If those giants are really creatures from Norse mythology, then it only makes sense they'd want something Norse mythological."

"Interesting phrasing. But go on."

"So what does Middleton have that would be valuable to something from the Norse myths?"

"The Middleton Stone," ABE said, catching on.

"Not just the Middleton Stone," Pru said, "but the treasure it's supposed to lead to. The Eye of Odin! Because if mythology is true, then the story we heard about the Eye of Odin might be true, too. It must be!"

"What story?" Mister Fox asked, his nose beginning to twitch.

Quickly, Pru and ABE told Mister Fox about their encounter with Ratatosk and Old Man Grimnir. Pru finished with the revelation that Old Man Grimnir had just one eye, himself.

"If what you've said about mythology is true, then could Old Man Grimnir really be . . . Odin?"

"It seems likely. Not many people could have told you that story. I have to admit, that's a fair bit of detective work you two accomplished. I'm almost impressed. Yes. I think that cinches it. The giant came here for the Middleton Stone. He wanted to use it to find the Eye of Odin. And if one came here looking for the stone, you can be sure others will come, too."

"But won't Mr. Grimnir . . . I mean Odin . . . stop them?" ABE asked.

"I'm not so sure. I'd heard rumors that Odin had grown reclusive. And he didn't do anything to stop the giant we met."

"What do we do, then?" Pru asked.

"I'm still working on that. But your question brings us back to ABE's point. Bureaus aren't just one person and I don't work alone. I need your help straightening things out here. You've already uncovered a lot without even knowing what you were looking for. So *keep* looking around. You know this town. Keep your eyes and ears open for anything unusual. You uncovered Odin. Who knows what else you might find. Report anything you discover back to me."

"Like Sherlock Holmes's Irregulars," Pru said,

remembering the stories her father had shared with her. "Sherlock Holmes used London's street urchins to gather information for him."

"Just so. Except I don't call my assistants Irregulars. I have a different name. Congratulations, Pru and ABE." The detective grinned, and the lantern light reflected off his teeth and sharp eyes. "You two just became Fibbers."

CHAPTER
15

ABE WAS PACING OUTSIDE THE FRONT DOORS OF THE school when Pru arrived Wednesday morning. She guessed from his anxious movement and the alarming state of his hair that he was upset about something.

"Pru! I've been waiting for you."

Pru's first thought had been that ABE was simply worked up over all they had learned the day before. Something about the way his eyes kept darting about in every direction suggested it was more than that, though.

"What's wrong?" she asked.

"I think we're trapped!"

Pru looked around. Kids hung about outside the school, enjoying their final moments of freedom before they'd be expected to go inside the gym and line up by class to start the day. Every once in a while, one would cast a nervous look at the ominous sky. Other than that, everything looked normal.

"I don't know, ABE. I'm having a hard time feeling intimidated by that group of kindergartners over there." Pru frowned, reconsidering. "Though some teacher really should wipe that one kid's nose. Ew."

"No, not here at school. I mean the whole town. Pru, I think we're surrounded."

"By what?"

ABE looked around him. Apparently satisfied no one would overhear, he replied, "Giants."

"What? What do you mean?"

"I stopped at the library last night on the way home. Everything Mister Fox said . . . well, it kind of shook me up and I find libraries relaxing. While I was there, I overheard a guy and a girl talking. They'd been at a place called the overlook. Do you know it?"

"Yeah. It's a spot along one of the hiking trails. It's a view of the valley that surrounds the town. Not that there's much to see," Pru said, shrugging. "Just a bunch of trees and the road that eventually goes to the highway."

ABE nodded. "That's kind of what I figured from the way the two were talking. Anyway, they'd been at the overlook, and they said the whole valley was filled with fog. I've been thinking. Mister Fox said the giant was a frost giant, right? Well, it's been pretty warm lately, except when the giant was around. Remember how cold it was the two times we saw him? It's like he radiated cold, which would make sense if he's a frost giant. Well, fog can form when warm air and cold air mix."

Pru didn't like where ABE was going with this. If fog formed around a frost giant, and the valley all around the town was filled with fog, it could really only mean one thing.

"Mister Fox was right," she said. "More giants have come looking for the Middleton Stone and the Eye of Odin."

"Pru, what are we going to do? Who knows how many giants are out there? Can Mister Fox get rid of them all with that looking glass of his? And why are they in the valley? Why haven't they tried to take the Middleton Stone?"

ABE's voice rose with every question, finally reaching a pitch that left Pru worried for the windows of the school.

"ABE, relax! It's going to be okay."

"It is?"

"Yes, it is. And do you know why?"

"No. Why?"

"Because," Pru said, straightening her shoulders and lifting her chin, "I have an idea."

❧

ABE had to wait until recess to hear Pru's plan. She almost didn't tell him even then. She hadn't appreciated how doubtful ABE had looked that morning when she'd first revealed that she *had* an idea for what they should do. He was going to have to learn to trust her. When had she ever led him astray?

Well, except for the time she'd led him into the woods and they'd been attacked by a giant. And the time she accidentally made him an accomplice to breaking and entering at Winterhaven House. And the time he'd followed her to the Fort of the Fallen only to get attacked by a giant.

Again.

Still. The point was he was going to have to learn to trust her.

And she *did* have a plan. It had come to her in the early hours of the morning.

"See," she began to explain at recess, "I was thinking about the same question you asked earlier. How come the giants haven't gone after the Middleton Stone? Mister Fox said that Odin wouldn't do anything to stop them. If Mister Fox knows that, the giants must know it, too. So I asked myself what they could be afraid of."

"And you came up with an answer?"

"Yeah! And it was so obvious. It's been right under our noses the whole time. Well, not exactly under our noses. More like over them."

"I'm not quite following."

"Do you remember that story we had to read for Mrs. Edleman? The one about Loki and Asgard's wall? Remember who the giant was afraid of in the story?"

ABE looked thoughtful for a moment. Then his eyes widened and he lifted his head to the sky—the sky that was filled with dark clouds and thunder.

"They were afraid of Thor," he said.

"Right! Thor . . . the *thunder* god. Think about it. Do you remember the first day we saw the giant? We were in the woods and he chased us. We didn't know what he was then, but he chased us into that clearing and you fell. I thought we were goners. But then, *KA-BOOM!*" Pru clapped, then immediately lowered her voice when a couple of nearby kids looked in her direction. "There was that big boom of thunder. I bet that's what spooked the giant off. The giants are scared of Thor. It said so in the story. And we've had all these thunderheads and all this thunder for days! I bet it's Thor. It's got to be!"

"That actually makes a lot of sense," ABE said. Pru did her best to ignore the surprise in ABE's voice. "But where is he?"

ABE looked around, as if he hoped to catch the thunder god hiding around a corner.

"That's the only part I haven't figured out yet. I mean, he's got to be nearby. He's in town somewhere, I just know it. All we have to do is find him."

✧

Pru would have liked to begin her search for the absent god of thunder that day, but she had a dentist appointment after school.

Driving home after the appointment (the dreaded, grainy texture of the dentist's ultramint toothpaste still in Pru's mouth), Pru's mother informed her that they had to stop by the police station to drop off the cans her office had collected for the station's food drive.

"Can't you go another time?" Pru said, fidgeting.

"I already took the afternoon off from work for your appointment, Pru. You know how busy I am these days. Look, sweetie, I know you don't like going to the station. You can wait in the car if you really don't want to go inside. But I really think it might be good for you to visit."

"That's okay. I'll wait outside."

Once they pulled into the parking lot, however, Pru found she couldn't resist the building's call. Taking her mother's cue and lifting a box of cans from the trunk, she walked through the front doors of the Middleton Police Department.

It didn't take long for Roger Lyons, who had been her dad's best friend, to find them once they went inside.

"I think you'll want to see this," Roger said to Pru as he led her and her mother through the busy squad room. Cheerful greetings met them at every step, and Pru had to dodge more than one attempt to ruffle her hair before they arrived at their destination, a quiet corner apparently reserved for old files and folders and things-not-quite-forgotten. There, half buried beneath mounds of paper, she saw it.

"Dad's desk," Pru said. Her mother and Roger hung back.

"They had it down in storage," Roger said. "I made them move it. It belongs up here where the action is."

Pru approached the desk. Behind her, she heard Roger say in an undertone to her mother, "How's she doing?"

"Okay." Her mother answered in a voice soft enough that Pru could barely hear. "She's still so angry, though. And she won't talk to me about anything."

Pru tuned the voices out and sat in the familiar seat that once belonged to her father. She wrapped her arms around the arms of his chair, safe for just that moment in its embrace. Then she reached out and read the scratches along the metal ridges of the desk with her fingertips.

Pru lived for such rare, stolen moments.

In moments like those, the world reset itself and felt the way it had before. Pru could almost convince herself that she had returned to another time as the familiar sensations conjured memories of sitting in that very chair, swinging her legs as she waited for her dad to get off duty. She could almost see him lean over a nearby desk, telephone receiver nestled on his shoulder as he jotted down notes from an incoming call.

"Pru," her mother interrupted in a soft voice, "Roger and I are going to chat in his office. Come join us when you're ready. Take as much time as you like."

Pru nodded and allowed herself the luxury of living in that other time for a few heartbeats longer. Then, closing her eyes, she let the moment slip away.

Her mother thought Pru avoided the station because it made her sad.

It did. But that wasn't why she avoided it. Sadness didn't keep her away, memories did. Memories lived in the station now, locked within walls of stone behind bars of steel. They weren't locked away from her, though. That's what her mother didn't understand. They were locked away *for* her, safe and untouched. Pru hated the cemetery because it reminded her of death. The station reminded her of life.

Pru avoided the station because moments like these

had to be rationed. Right now, the desk and chair belonged to another time and had the power to return her to that time, however briefly. If she lingered too long, they'd become a fixture in this world without a dad and they'd lose that power.

Best to move on.

Pru rose and returned to the present, though she allowed her fingertips to linger on the back of the chair for as long as possible as she stepped away. Her one arm reached back to the past, yearning to hold on.

When she finally did let go, Pru made a beeline for the water fountain. The light spray from the nozzle hit her face as the cold water ran down her throat. She stood up, free to bury her face for a moment in the sleeve of her coat to wipe the excess moisture away.

Not quite ready to go find her mother, Pru made her way to the stairs that led to the lockup area where she'd find the bulletin board with the WANTED posters. She liked to know what she was up against. As she descended the stairs, she crossed her fingers that she'd know the officer on duty. Otherwise, she'd just get sent away. She was in luck.

"Hi, Sergeant Mahoney," she said as she reached the bottom of the steps.

"Prudence Potts," the rotund man behind the desk said. His bushy mustache wriggled when he talked, like a furry black caterpillar that was eager to crawl off. "It's finally happened, hasn't it? You've landed yourself in lockup. What did you do?"

He held up his hands, silencing her.

"No. Wait. Don't tell me. I don't want to know. I prefer to remember you as the sweet, innocent child you were. Although"—he paused and adopted a thoughtful expression—"I'm not sure my memory goes back that far."

Slowly, and with great purpose and dignity, Pru stuck out her tongue.

"Get over here, ruffian. It's about time you came to visit us. What's the occasion?"

"I came with my mom." Pru surrendered to another hair ruffle. As she did, her eyes chanced upon the door to the lockup area. "Has anyone interesting come through lately?"

"Prudence, you're a snoop and a scoundrel. Lucky for you, that's half your charm. But, no. Sorry to disappoint, little lady, but it's been quiet as ever here. Although . . ." Sergeant Mahoney's pupils narrowed and his face assumed a distracted expression. "Hold on. Now that you mention it, there was that one gent."

"Who?"

"You know, I don't think we ever got his name. That's odd, though, isn't it?" Beads of sweat formed on the sergeant's forehead as though it were an effort for him to remember. "We should have gotten his name. There are forms and such. He was some drifter, I suppose. Dressed real funny. That's right, we figured him to be a volunteer for the fair, dressed the way he was."

"How was he dressed?"

"Who?" The sergeant blinked at Pru, as though he'd already forgotten she was there. "Oh, right, that gent in lockup. Well, he was dressed like a Viking. Weird, huh? The joker must have gotten drunk and put on his costume for the Explorers' Fair. We picked him up in the woods, out by that old fort. Got a tip from Old Man Grimnir, of all people."

Pru faked a cough to cover the look of surprise on her face. "What happened to this guy?" she asked, trying not to sound too interested.

Without turning his head, Sergeant Mahoney glanced quickly toward the door to the holding cells.

He looked quickly away.

"Is he still here? That can't be, though, can it? When did we pick him up? Was it late Wednesday?" He tugged at his collar. "Is it hot in here?"

"Um, a little," Pru said. Sergeant Mahoney's distracted behavior seemed familiar. It reminded Pru of her mother's reaction when Pru tried to show her Mister Fox's envelope. Mister Fox had said that people who couldn't see magic had a hard time focusing on the envelopes. Did that mean that Sergeant Mahoney was having a hard time focusing because *the prisoner* was magic, too? Was he a Mythic?

"If you're hot, why don't you go get some water?" Pru suggested. "My mom's upstairs. I'm sure she'd love to see you."

"I can't, really. Must stay at my post, you know. Duty first." The sergeant seemed unaware that he'd risen to his feet.

"Sure you can. It's not like anyone's going anywhere. Right?"

"Right." Sergeant Mahoney laughed nervously. He appeared eager to get away. "Coming?"

"In a sec," Pru said. She pointed to the bulletin board with the wanted posters. "Gotta study up. It's been a while, you know?"

"Of course, of course." The sergeant waved absently and then hiked his pants as he climbed the stairs.

Pru watched him go. Then, before she could talk herself out of it, she slid her hand under the duty desk and pressed the button she wasn't supposed to know about. It unlocked the door leading to the cells. She dashed through and entered the hallway beyond.

Her footfalls echoed off the cement floor and walls as she made her way to the first cell. The air tingled with electricity.

Empty.

Swallowing her disappointment, Pru continued. The shadows deepened, unaffected by the pitiful light that managed to penetrate the heavy clouds and enter the shallow basement window wells. Pru felt the hairs on the back of her neck lift as the contents of the second cell came into view.

Those contents turned out to be neither mysterious nor mythological. Neat stacks of canned goods stood in ordered piles, waiting for the Explorers' Fair.

Small, hesitant steps carried Pru to the third and final cell—and its lone occupant. Pru clasped her hand over her mouth to keep from crying out in surprise.

If the being in the cell was who Pru thought he must be, it was no wonder Middleton was covered with dark, brooding clouds and skies filled with angry thunder. The man was big and hairy and looked a bit like how Pru imagined a bear would look if someone were to dress it up like a Viking and then stick a beard on it. If Pru was right, the man locked up in the third holding cell of the Middleton Police Department was Thor, the Norse god of thunder.

And, boy, did he look mad.

CHAPTER 16

JUDGING BY THE SIZE AND OVERALL ANGRY BEAR-ness of the prisoner, Pru wasn't at all sure she wanted to approach him. She had seen a movie once in which a boxer swallowed whole eggs to help him bulk up. The man in the cell didn't look like he swallowed whole eggs. He looked like he swallowed whole chickens.

No.

He looked like he swallowed whole boxers.

"You're him, aren't you?" Pru asked as soon as she mustered the courage. "You're Thor."

She thought she saw an eyebrow rise, but it was hard to tell in the tangle of red hair that covered the man's face. Only his blazing green eyes showed clearly. They glinted like the sun reflecting off metal.

"I'm impressed," Thor said. Pru was surprised to hear a hint of gentleness in the gruff rumble of his voice. In the next moment, his face fell. "Very few people of Midgard see me these days. Far fewer recognize me."

If Pru hadn't known better, she'd have said the mighty god of thunder sounded a bit like he was moping.

"I've had a lot of practice recognizing Norse gods, lately. I think I sort of met your dad," she added, edging closer.

Thor's eyes blazed at that and Pru took a step back. Then she took another.

"Odin is still here on Midgard?" Thor asked.

"Yeah. He spends a lot of time here, I think. He's even got a house."

"A house?" Thor's face twisted into an expression of deep thought. It did not seem to be an expression with which he was very comfortable or familiar. "My father had me imprisoned because I came to Midgard against his wishes. Why would he keep a house here?"

"I don't know . . . Wait. Your dad got you arrested? How come?"

Thor looked away as the sky outside rumbled in a way that sounded suspiciously like someone clearing his throat awkwardly. His shoulders slumped.

"It's, ah, possible that I disobeyed him. A little," Thor said.

"Really? What did you do?"

"My duty!" Thor thundered. "Long ago, when our worlds began to grow apart, my father ordered that we of Asgard stay away from Midgard. I obeyed him for hundreds of your years. But when word reached me recently that a raiding party of frost giants had come here, I knew I had to do something."

"That's right," Pru said, remembering the story she and ABE had read. "You used to protect Earth, or, ah, Midgard, didn't you?"

"I did." Thor sat up a bit straighter. "So I felt honor bound to come here and see to the giants. I had hoped that, well . . ."

"You hoped that you could sneak out of Asgard, whack a few giants in the head with your hammer, and get back home before your dad found out?" Pru found herself warming to Thor.

The mighty god of thunder shifted on the bench. The sky grumbled again.

"Well . . . yes. I suppose. Something like that. But it was a foolish hope. There's very little my father doesn't see. He caught me before I could find the giants and told me that if I loved the mortal world so much that I would disobey him, then I should enjoy its hospitality for a time. He ordered me to serve out my punishment here." Thor gestured to his cell.

"He grounded you. That stinks," Pru said, feeling

instant empathy and a sense of kinship. Then she frowned. "But wait. I don't get it. Why would he do that? If the giants aren't stopped, they're going to stomp my town. And they'll get the Eye of Odin."

"*WHAT?*" The sky outside roared, and Thor was on his feet, his fists clenching the bars of his door. Pru never even saw him move. "Explain what you just said!"

"The Eye of Odin," Pru sputtered, staggering back and pressing against the damp, cool wall. "Odin wrote the hiding place of the Eye of Odin on a rune stone, and that stone is here. That's why the giants are in Middleton. They're after the Eye."

"*WHAT?*" Thor repeated, and the whole building quaked as thunder filled the air. Thor shook his fists and the two bars he held broke free, spilling concrete rubble across the floor. Startled, Thor looked at the twisted bars in his hands. A sheepish expression replaced the anger on his face.

"Er, sorry," he mumbled. "Bit of a temper." He leaned the now-loose bars against their neighbors in an awkward and unsuccessful attempt to disguise what he'd done. Glancing at the ruined cell door, he folded his hands behind his back in an I-didn't-do-it gesture.

"I am just surprised," he said, after taking a deep breath. "And . . . confused. I knew my father was consumed with thoughts of Ragnarok, but I never thought he would allow the Eye of Odin to be found. Ever since he drank from the Well of Wisdom, his manner has changed. He never *acts* anymore. He just watches!"

"Ragnarok," Pru repeated. "I've heard of that. It's supposed to be some big battle, right?"

"It is more than that. It is the final battle. When Ragnarok comes, Loki will lead his army of frost giants against the gods of Asgard, and our battle will destroy all of the three worlds."

"Wait. All of them?" Pru hated to sound selfish, but she had to ask. "Even . . . even my world? Even Midgard?"

"Even so." Thor's expression softened. "But keep in mind, little one, my father foresaw that this would happen, but he did not see when. Time passes differently in Asgard than it does in your mortal world. Hundreds of thousands of years could pass here before Ragnarok strikes. At least, that had always been my hope. But this news about the Eye of Odin worries me. If the Eye is the prize here, the giants are not the real trouble."

"They kind of seem like trouble to me."

The sky echoed the soft rumble of Thor's laughter.

"Frost giants are brutes. They prefer action, not strategy. It's one of the few things I like about them. They bash and smash, none of that troublesome thinking. They don't care about the Eye of Odin. That prize has always been the desire of another. If the giants are here seeking the Eye, then there is someone else here, too, guiding their actions."

"Who?" Pru asked.

"Loki."

"The one who starts Ragnarok? And wait," Pru said, remembering another story, "isn't he the one who got Asgard's wall built, too?"

"He did. Loki has always been the cleverest among us. Not the wisest, mind you, but always the most clever."

"You talk about him like he's your friend."

"He is."

"How can you say that? He's going to destroy both our worlds!"

"Someday, yes. But for now, Loki only brings mischief. And sometimes his mischief brings great reward."

"So . . . he's not bad?"

"Not yet. Well, not completely. But I'm afraid everything will change if Loki gets the Eye of Odin. Right now, Loki believes he can change his fate."

"Good for him! Maybe he can."

Thor shook his head. "Perhaps mortals can change their future. I don't know. But gods have a different relationship with the fates. We are bound. My father has seen it. If Loki looks into the Eye of Odin, he will see himself revealed as the villain he must become. I am afraid that will push him to the very acts that will doom us all and bring about Ragnarok."

"Okay," Pru said, shivering. "We need to keep Loki away from the Eye of Odin. But, I mean, you're Thor. Look at what you did to those bars. You can break out of here and smash those giants into dust!"

And she could show off to Mister Fox and ABE by claiming the credit for finding Thor. Not that getting credit for saving the day was the most important thing, Pru reminded herself.

(But it sort of was.)

"I can't, little one," Thor said, bringing Pru's inner celebration to an instant and terrible halt. "I'm sorry."

"What do you mean?"

Thor looked down at his booted feet. For a moment the Viking god of thunder reminded Pru, impossibly, of ABE.

"I can't disobey my father again. Odin says we must not interfere with Midgard. I was wrong not to listen. He is the Father of Wisdom while I . . . Well, I am not famous for my thinking." Thor glanced at the ruined bars.

"But you're our only chance. You're the only one the giants are afraid of, the only one strong enough to beat them!"

Thor puffed his chest out, clearly pleased. Pru thought that he might change his mind for a moment, but he quickly deflated.

"I can*not* disobey my father again. *I will not.* I must remain here until my father releases me, then I must return to Asgard. And yet . . ." Thor's face took on a pained expression. "Perhaps there is another way to stop Loki."

"What?" Pru said, stepping closer again.

"My father commanded that everyone from Asgard stay away from Midgard." Thor spoke slowly as he labored to give birth to an idea. "That command applies to Loki, too. I am sure Loki is here, guiding the giants. If you find him and expose him to my father, Odin will be forced to finally take some action. He will punish Loki as he has punished me. Without Loki's guidance, the giants will return to Jotunheim."

"But I don't get it. If Loki is here in Middleton, how come Odin hasn't punished him already?"

"Because Loki can be very hard to find. He is called the Sly One, the Lord of Lies. Even his appearance can lie. He's a shape-shifter."

"A shape-shifter?" Pru slumped. "So he could be anyone?"

"No. Not anyone. There is nothing that Loki enjoys so much as being clever, and he never feels so clever as when he is making someone else feel foolish. Loki will be at the very center of things here in your town, the truth of his identity buried in lies. And since you also appear to be at the center of things, little one, I would guess that Loki is someone you've already met, someone close to you. That's the thing about Loki. He may be your greatest enemy, but he can appear to you as the closest of friends."

Pru's face darkened and Thor sighed again before continuing.

"This is a heavy burden I'm asking you to carry. But Loki cannot be allowed to find the Eye of Odin. It appears you are the only one in a position to stop him. And I"—Thor looked suddenly embarrassed—"I haven't even asked your name."

"I'm Pru."

Thor reached into a pouch tied to his belt and withdrew what appeared to be a necklace.

"I greet you, Pru. It used to be that the people of Midgard would carry an amulet like this, fashioned in the shape of my hammer, Mjolnir, around their necks. They wore it and called on me in times of need. Though I can't do anything to help you stop Loki, I'd like you to have this, anyway, as a sign of my favor." Thor handed the necklace to Pru through the bars.

"Thanks," Pru mumbled, preoccupied by what Thor had said. It wasn't just that he wouldn't help. Thor had said that Loki could appear as one of her closest friends. That news wouldn't have bothered Pru a couple of weeks earlier. She hadn't had any friends. Not really. Now, though, she had two.

Or so she'd thought.

The idea that ABE or Mister Fox might not be who she thought he was tormented Pru as she rejoined her mother and they returned home. The worst part, Pru found herself thinking in bed that night as darkness and doubt settled in, was that she didn't know who she wanted to be the liar. ABE was the first friend she'd had in school in a very long time. She wasn't sure exactly when she'd begun thinking of him as a friend. Now, the very real possibility that he might *not* be her friend upset her more than she wanted to admit.

Then there was Mister Fox. Even though his tendency to be amused by everything (especially her) annoyed Pru, she found him intriguing. And he'd opened her eyes to whole new worlds.

But had he?

Doubt crept closer. Hadn't she and ABE already begun to figure out that magic and mythology were real when they met Old Man Grimnir? Pru tried to think of anything that Mister Fox had told them that she and ABE hadn't already known. Sure, he had shown them the Henhouse and told them the story about Baba Yaga. But who knew if any of it was true? Maybe he made up the story with Baba Yaga. Maybe all that stuff about people finding their own answers just gave Mister Fox an excuse to discourage her and ABE from asking too many questions.

Or was she letting ABE off the hook too easily?

Pru tossed restlessly, becoming as tangled in her covers as she was in her thoughts. She remembered one of the first things Mister Fox had said to ABE in the Henhouse—that ABE was lying about his name. Had Mister Fox been right, after all? Wasn't it suspicious that ABE arrived in town at the same time the giants appeared? Wouldn't his family have moved for the start of the school year? Come to think of it, did ABE even have a family? Pru couldn't remember him ever talking about his parents or anyone else.

Then again, she couldn't remember ever asking him, either.

It was a long time before Pru fell asleep. When sleep finally did claim her, she had fewer answers, and far more questions, than she'd begun with.

⬠

Pru avoided ABE as much as she could on Thursday. She didn't make eye contact in the hallway when everyone put their bags in their lockers. She hung back when it was time to line up for lunch so she could see where in the cafeteria ABE sat. Then she tried to ignore his wounded, puppy-dog look when, for the first time since they'd met, she sat somewhere else.

There was no avoiding him at recess, though.

"Hi," he said, walking over to her with his thumbs

hooked in his belt loops and his eyes downcast. "Uh, is everything okay?"

"Yeah. Sure. Why wouldn't it be?"

"I don't know. Um, how were things at the dentist?"

"Good." Pru peered at him. "Why do you ask?"

"I don't know. Just wondering? I mean, we found out all this amazing stuff the other day. Then you had your appointment yesterday, and I haven't had anyone to talk to about it all. Anyone else would think I'm crazy, or something. By the way, I looked around town yesterday after school for Thor while I collected recyclables. I couldn't find him."

Pru glanced at the clouds overhead and thought of her discovery of Thor. She wished she could tell ABE all about it. But could she trust him? She felt even less sure standing there than she had the night before. Since she couldn't just ask ABE if he was trustworthy, she took a different approach.

"What do you think of Mister Fox?" she asked.

"Oh. Well, he's . . . different."

"What does that mean? You don't like him?"

"No. I mean, yes. Well, sort of. I don't know." ABE took a deep breath. "This is going to sound stupid, but when I was little—well, littler—we used to play this game at my old school called What Time Is It, Mr. Fox? I know the name is just coincidence, but it's the first thing I thought of when he told us what to call him. Anyway, in the game, everyone would line up on one side of a field, shoulder to shoulder. Then we'd all ask, 'What time is it, Mr. Fox?' The teacher, who played Mr. Fox, would say a time. If he said, 'Three o'clock,' then we'd take three steps. We'd get closer and closer each turn, until Mr. Fox yelled 'Midnight!' and started chasing everyone. The thing is, I always hated that game. It was like the teacher suddenly turned into someone else, someone scary."

Pru frowned. She'd played a variation of the game in gym class. Her teacher had called it What Time Is It, Mr. Wolf? Did the fact that ABE talked about his other school and the games he played there mean he was who he said he was . . . or was he just a really good liar?

"Mister Fox—the real Mister Fox—reminds me of that game," ABE continued. "It's not just the name. There's something about him. He's great, I guess. He's amazing, anyway. But there's something that doesn't feel quite safe about him. I'm not sure I trust him."

"He saved our lives that day at the fort," Pru said, suddenly defensive.

"I know, I know," ABE said, nodding. But then, more quietly, he added, "But if you think about it, he also used us as bait. He drew the giant's attention to us so we could lure him to Mister Fox."

"You don't know what you're talking about." Pru, who had just been considering the possibility that Mister Fox might not be who he pretended to be, found herself growing angry.

"Sorry." ABE flinched at Pru's tone. "I . . . I know you must like him because he's a detective like your dad—"

"What?" Pru sucked in her breath. "Who told you about that?"

"It's a small town. I'm sorry. I just . . . I wanted you to know . . ." ABE sighed. "I'm just sorry."

"You want to know what I think? I think you don't like Mister Fox because he scares you. It has nothing to do with trust. You just want to not like him because he reminds you of all the stuff that's going on that terrifies you and makes you speak in your scaredy-cat, high-pitched voice." Pru did her best imitation of ABE's frightened squeak. "So much for Aloysius, the *famous warrior.*"

ABE ducked his head and hunched his shoulders forward like a turtle retreating into its shell.

"I'm not going to make it to the Earth Center today," Pru finished. "I'm not feeling good. I guess lunch or *something* disagreed with me, so I'm going to go home after school."

With that, Pru walked away from ABE. She didn't look back.

CHAPTER 17

PRU WOKE UP FRIDAY MORNING RESOLVED TO TAKE action. She had no idea what that action should be, but she was resolved to take it.

She was so focused on figuring out what to do while she ate her breakfast that she almost didn't hear the news report that came on the television moments before she left for school. Normally, the words "breaking news" and "robbery" would have captured her attention instantly. Now, she had bigger mysteries to solve.

Inspiration struck as Pru walked to school. If she couldn't figure out on her own who was lying, then her best chance would be to get Mister Fox and ABE together and confront them both. That way, at least,

Loki would be outnumbered. It was risky (the sensible part of Pru's brain shouted that it was reckless), but Pru *had* to do something. Giants were out there in the woods and could attack at any time. Thor's thunder wouldn't keep them away forever.

Pru plotted the best ways to avoid ABE until she could put her plan into action. It turned out she needn't have bothered. ABE remained absent as her class settled in for morning announcements. Pru felt an awful, empty sort of feeling begin to grow in her stomach. The feeling grew worse as the morning pressed on and it became clear that ABE wouldn't be in school at all. She wasn't sure if it was guilt over being mean to ABE the day before or suspicion about where he was—all she knew was she felt sick.

When school ended, Pru served her final day of detention with Mrs. Edleman. Each second that ticked by seemed like an eternity. She had decided sometime during math that she would go to the Earth Center after school and see if ABE was there. If he was, she would still try to act on her plan. If he wasn't . . . Pru didn't know what she'd do.

When her time was up, Pru nearly knocked her desk over in her hurry to leave the classroom. Mrs. Edleman called Pru to her desk, though, before she made it to the door.

"I hope you've learned something from this,

Prudence," her teacher said, looking at Pru over her reading glasses.

Pru nodded, not trusting herself to speak.

"These investigations of yours simply must stop." Mrs. Edleman put the cap on the pen she'd been using to mark papers and, after carefully setting the pen aside, folded her hands on her desk. "This has all gone on quite long enough, young lady. Let me tell you what I think. I think we have all been too soft on you, Prudence Potts. What happened to your father was . . . is . . . tragic."

For just a moment, sympathy showed on Mrs. Edleman's face. That just made the tightness that had suddenly gripped Pru's chest all the worse.

"But since then, I fear the adults in your life have been far too indulgent. It is time for the truth. You are a child, Prudence. You are *not* a detective, and it is time for you to put these absurd investigations of yours behind you once and for all. *I* care too much about your future to permit this ridiculous charade to continue. Do we understand each other?"

Pru's cheeks burned so hot she was sure that flames would shoot out from her mouth if she opened it.

"I'll take your silence as a yes, then. Your mother left a message with the office," Mrs. Edleman said, handing Pru a blue slip of paper that read *Change of Dismissal* at the top. "Apparently, you're to go straight home today. You'll be excused from your community service. You may go. Have a nice weekend."

Pru arrived at the Earth Center a short time later, her face still burning. She had to see if ABE was there. Then she'd go straight home.

Most people stepped out of her way when they saw her. A few of them had, possibly, heard of her skill with her elbows and knew from the look on her face not to get too close. One person did not know better.

"Pru, I wonder if we could talk for a moment?" Fay said, and, reluctantly, Pru followed the woman into her office. There had been no sign of ABE.

Fay straightened her shoulders as she closed the door behind them, but they slumped almost immediately as a look of regret showed on her face. "Pru, I hate to do this, but I have to be honest with you. I'm afraid I'm not going to be able to sign your community service slip."

"What? What do you mean?" Pru was so upset by Mrs. Edleman and worried about ABE's absence that it took her a moment to understand what Fay was talking about.

"I'm sorry, Pru," Fay said, wringing her hands. "But what can I do? You were supposed to spend a week with the recycling drive. You've only come half of the time, and even on the days you've been here, you haven't come back with any recyclables. *None.*"

Pru squirmed in her chair. If Mrs. Edleman found out—if her mom found out!—that she hadn't been doing her volunteer work, there would be more detention and more talks.

"Please, Fay, I'm sorry. I really am. It's been a hard week. I swear, I'll make it up to you. I'll do extra volunteer work. I'll do anything."

"Pru, I like you. I really, really do. But I can't lie for you." Fay bit her lower lip, and Pru saw in the gesture a glimmer of hope. She knew hesitation on sight.

"*Please*, Fay," she pressed.

"Oh dear. Pru, I can't. Don't you understand? I have no idea where you've been or what you've been doing all week. What if you're doing something dangerous? I couldn't live with myself if I lied for you and you got hurt—"

"It's not like that," Pru interrupted, knowing she was close to losing Fay. "It's just, I've been going . . . to the cemetery."

The words were out before Pru could stop them.

"The cemetery?" Fay said, startled. "Whatever for, dear?"

Pru closed her eyes. She hated using her dad in a lie. But she had to say something now, and she couldn't tell Fay about Mister Fox.

"My dad's buried there." Pru chose her words carefully, keeping as close to the truth as she could.

"Oh, Pru. I didn't know. I'm so sorry," Fay said, cupping her hand to her mouth and speaking through her fingers.

"It's okay. I mean, it's not, but . . . It happened last year. My dad ran to the store at the gas station to get something for my mom. There was a guy there with a gun. My dad was a detective, but he wasn't even on duty that night." Pru closed her eyes and took a deep, shuddering breath. "He just tried to help."

She felt Fay's hand on her shoulder.

"Pru, I haven't the words to say how sorry I am. But there's no reason to sneak off to visit your father's grave. I'm sure your mother would take you to his grave anytime you'd like."

Pru opened her eyes and pulled away.

"You don't understand. My mom always tries to talk about things, like that's going to make it better. Like I can even believe what she says. I can't believe what anyone says." Pru pressed the palms of her hands to her temples, desperate to keep all the thoughts that were jumble-banging about her brain contained.

"I might understand better than you think. Relationships between mothers and children are complicated."

Pru looked up at that. "You're a mom?"

"I am. Though motherhood came to me unexpectedly, and it saddens me to say that I gave my child to someone else to raise shortly after his birth. But this isn't about me," Fay said. "We're talking about you, and I have an offer to make you. I will sign your slip for school. Honoring the memory of a good man, a hero, seems like a service to the community to me. But there is one condition. I want you to promise me that you will think about telling your mother about your trips to the cemetery. You may be surprised by what comes from the conversation."

"Okay," Pry said instantly, "I promise I'll think about it."

"*Really* think about it."

"Fine. I'll *really* think about it," Pru said, surprised to find that she really was considering it.

"Good. I'm glad. Now, then. I haven't seen your partner in crime yet. Is ABE coming today?"

"I don't know." The momentary relief Pru had felt slipped away. "We kind of got into an argument yesterday."

"Oh dear. Can I help?"

"No. No one can. It's just . . . I know one of my friends is lying to me, only I don't know who." Pru expected Fay to jump to ABE's defense. Instead, a look of surprise crossed the woman's face.

"What is it?" Pru asked her.

"What? No, I'm sure it's nothing," Fay said, but she looked troubled. "ABE is such a good boy."

"Fay, please . . ."

With a sigh, Fay gestured for Pru to wait a moment and then stepped into another room. She returned carrying a notebook.

"ABE left this behind yesterday. I didn't mean to read it, but he left it open. I happened to see what he'd written at the bottom of the page."

Pru took the notebook. There at the bottom, beneath a line of crossed-out text and written neatly in ABE's handwriting, were the words *I AM OFTEN LYING.* Pru felt a chill pass through her worse than anything she'd felt in the presence of a frost giant.

"I have to go," she said. She had to get to Mister Fox. "You can get rid of the notebook. I don't think ABE will be back for it."

CHAPTER 18

PRU RAN ALL THE WAY FROM THE ABANDONED church to the cemetery. Then she hit a wall.

In fact, she hit four walls.

When Pru arrived at the Henhouse, she discovered once again that the ramshackle building did not appear to have a door. She circled the Henhouse twice, just to be sure. The same thing had happened on her first visit, she remembered. She hadn't been able to find a door that time, either. Not at first. Then *something* had happened and the entrance just appeared.

What had happened? Pru concentrated, trying to remember.

A memory of creaking wood and rustling feathers

came to mind. Just before those sounds, Mister Fox had said something. Only he hadn't spoken the words out loud. He'd whispered them. Pru remembered his lips moving in a silent incantation.

She hadn't thought much about it at the time. There had been too much happening. Now, Pru scrunched her eyes shut and tried to re-create the moment. She pictured the movement of Mister Fox's mouth and tried to read his lips from memory.

What was it he'd said?

There was something about a house. A little house. He'd repeated that.

Little house, little house . . .

Then what? He'd asked the house to hear something. It had started with a *p*. Pru recognized the positioning of the lips from having practiced speaking her own name while looking in a mirror so many times.

Little house, little house, hear my please . . .

No. That didn't make sense.

That was the problem with reading lips. You could only get so much from the way a person moved their mouth. Sometimes, you had to guess the rest depending on what made sense.

Pru thought about the rest of what she'd seen. The last bit came easily. He'd asked the little house to turn from the woods and look at him. She remembered because when the house *had* turned to reveal its door and its single round window, Pru had thought the window looked like an eye.

Little house, little house, hear my . . . something. Turn from the woods and look at me.

There was something singsongy about the words. Maybe the two sentences were meant to rhyme?

Just like that, she had it. Still with her eyes closed and picturing Mister Fox while she repeated his whispered words, she spoke aloud: "Little house, little house, hear my *plea*. Turn from the woods and look at me!"

A rustling sound filled the air, something between creaking wood and the ruffling of feathers. When Pru opened her eyes, the entrance to the Henhouse stood in front of her. Pru threw open the double doors and rushed inside, keeping pace as the arched hallway opened up before her, door after door. She burst through the final set of doors prepared to shout for Mister Fox, but as she entered the central chamber of the Henhouse, the words died on her lips.

Darkness seeped down from the vaulted heights above, and an eerie wind blew through the empty hall. It filled the space with a soft, haunting whine. Only a few lanterns were lit, and those burned dimly. The scene looked very different than it had on her first visit, when the space had been filled with an inviting glow.

Among the pillars of trees, Pru felt once again like

she stood in an ancient forest. Only this time she felt like she stood there at night, alone, which was a very different sort of thing.

She considered leaving right then, but a soft thud from somewhere overhead held her in place. A door on the level above her creaked open. Pru thought she saw a shadow pass across the opening.

"Mister Fox?" Pru called.

She meant to call, anyway. The words came out in a nervous whisper.

"Mister Fox?" Pru said again, a little more loudly. The words echoed through the cavernous chamber. No one answered.

Pru began to walk slowly toward the room upstairs. It took her a moment to find her way. The first set of stairs wasn't quite where she remembered it. Eventually, she made her way up (she didn't remember the stairs creaking quite so much the last time) and approached the open door.

"Mister Fox? It's me, Pru. Are you in here?"

The room beyond the door turned out to be a library. In keeping with the unusual design of the Henhouse, the library was a mystery in itself, a riddle of overflowing bookshelves and aisles. Pru wandered the labyrinth of shelves and worktables, all of which were covered with maps, diagrams, and open books with more dog-ears than a litter of puppies.

In a far corner of the room, on a long wooden table that was scratched and pitted with age, Pru found a stone, about the size of a dinner plate and covered with strange markings. She had seen the stone twice before.

At first, she couldn't wrap her mind around it. How could the Middleton Stone be inside the Henhouse? Only then, remembering a half-heard news report about a robbery, did she begin to understand the truth.

Mister Fox had stolen the Middleton Stone.

But why?

An answer presented itself, there in the house in the cemetery. It shambled up from the depths of her mind like a zombie from the grave. Fox the Fibber and Loki the liar. Were they the same person, after all? Had Pru been wrong about ABE?

For a long moment, confusion froze Pru in place. Then a sudden noise from outside the door spurred her into action. She swept up the Middleton Stone and slipped it into her messenger bag before doubling back and hiding herself within the maze of bookcases near the entrance to the library.

Mister Fox tore into the room. The anger Pru saw on his face as she peered between shelves terrified her.

"Where are you?" he shouted. "I know you're here. There's no use hiding. Come out!"

Pru didn't know how he knew she was in the

Henhouse. But he *did* know, and he was furious. She held her breath.

Instead of turning in Pru's direction, Mister Fox did just as Pru had hoped he would. He set off toward the back of the library, where Pru had discovered the Middleton Stone. She raced for the door as soon as he was out of sight.

Her luck held long enough for her to find her way back to the stairs and down to the first level without any trouble. Then luck abandoned her. She was half-way to the front door when a shout caused her to spin back in the direction of the library.

"You!" the man called Mister Fox howled from the level above. He towered over her, his hands clenched on the railing as he glared down.

Pru didn't wait around to hear anything else. She took off at a sprint. As she passed the lanterns that hung on either side of the exit, she swung her messenger bag with all her might. The lanterns shattered in a satisfying shower of sparks.

Still running at full speed, Pru escaped into the cemetery. She raced through the growing darkness, wondering how much of a head start her stunt with the lanterns had given her. She didn't have to wait long for her answer.

As she crested a hill that would lead her to the road

through the cemetery, Pru glanced back. She immediately wished she hadn't. Mister Fox was out of the Henhouse and running full speed in her direction. It wasn't fair! His legs were so long!

Pru ran on, but as she neared the bottom of the hill, a sense of futility weighed her down even more than the increasingly heavy stone in her messenger bag. She would never make it. Even if she somehow got to the main road, the town was at least a mile away. Mister Fox would catch her long before she got there. What would he do to her?

The darkness around Pru deepened quickly, the way it often does on an autumn night. Pru was feeling close to surrender when she spotted a car and hope surged.

Its headlights shone like twin beacons to Pru as she dashed toward them. She didn't know who was in the car. She didn't care! At that point, she'd have been happy to see Mrs. Edleman herself driving.

Pru waved to get the driver's attention. The car slowed to a stop and the driver's side window lowered. Pru lurched to a halt as she recognized the person in the car.

"Fay!" She'd never been so happy to see anyone in her whole entire life.

"Pru, *STOP*!"

The voice from behind froze Pru with its force. She

turned to find her pursuer standing at the top of the hill she'd just descended, framed by the raging sky behind him. He held the fox-head looking glass in his hand.

"Pru, stop!" he repeated. "Do not get into that car! Do you hear me? *DO NOT GET INTO THAT CAR!*"

Shaking off her shock at seeing him so close, Pru sprinted around to the passenger side as Fay reached across to open the door.

"Pru, what's wrong? Are you okay? Who is that man?"

"He's a liar and a thief and we have to go! Please, Fay. Drive!"

Looking troubled but nodding, Fay shifted into drive and the car rolled forward.

"Faster!" Pru urged. They weren't safe yet. The road was too narrow to turn around on. They had to follow it deeper into the cemetery before it would circle around and lead them back out and to safety. She craned her neck in one direction, then another, looking for signs of pursuit as they drove. "Hurry!"

"Pru, you're scaring me. What's going on?"

They rounded the final bend. The main gate stood before them.

"Please, just drive, Fay. I'll explain later. I promise." Pru clutched her messenger bag to her chest. They were thirty yards away from the gate. Twenty.

He burst onto the road ahead. His coat flared out behind him, making him seem even larger than he was.

"STOP!" he bellowed.

Fay slowed.

"Fay, no!" Pru grabbed the woman's sleeve. "Don't stop. You can't stop."

"Pru, I—"

"Please, Fay. Trust me! I know I haven't always been honest before. I know! But please, just this once—you have to believe me. Just this once. You can't stop, I swear!" Pru willed Fay to listen to her. She didn't care if anyone ever believed her again. Just this once!

Fay looked torn for a moment. Then her hands tightened on the steering wheel and her foot pressed down on the gas. The car leapt forward and the man Pru thought had been her friend had no choice but to dive out of the way or be run down.

Turning in her seat, Pru saw him roll to his feet and begin to run after them, but there was nothing he could do. The car had reached the gate and was turning onto the main road. Soon, they'd pick up speed and be gone. Her last glimpse of him was as they turned the corner. He was shouting her name.

CHAPTER 19

FINALLY ABLE TO RELAX, PRU LOOSENED HER DEATH grip on her messenger bag and reached inside. She pulled out the Middleton Stone, relieved to see that she hadn't broken it when she'd swung it against the lanterns.

She'd done it. She'd escaped.

Better.

She'd stopped Loki.

"Pru, what's going on. Who was that man?"

"He was a thief." Pru didn't want to lie to Fay, not after the woman had just saved her. But Fay would never believe the whole story. She gestured to the Middleton Stone. "He stole this from Winterhaven House."

"I don't understand. How did you get it?"

"I was in the cemetery," Pru began, choosing her words carefully. "I found an old shack. Inside, I found this. I knew it was stolen. It was on the news this morning. So when I saw it, I took it. But the thief—that man—almost caught me. I barely got away."

"How did he know your name?"

"I met him at the museum on my school field trip." That was technically true. "He must have been casing the place."

"That man . . . Pru, did he hurt you?"

"No." Pru shook her head. "You saved me."

"Not me, Pru, your mother. She called the Earth Center worried when you didn't show up at your house. Apparently, she'd heard about the robbery and was afraid you'd go on what she called one of your investigations." Fay gave Pru a look that balanced disappointment and hurt perfectly. "You didn't tell me you were supposed to go straight home from school today. Luckily, I knew where you were going."

"You're not going to tell my mom what happened, are you?"

"No," Fay said, and Pru breathed a sigh of relief. "Because I'm going to give you the chance to tell her first. *Then* I'm going to tell her, if you don't."

"But—"

"Pru, listen." Fay's voice sounded gentle. It sounded concerned. But it also sounded very firm. "Something terrible could have happened to you today. You can't keep sneaking off and wandering about. You and your mother need to talk, so that's what you're going to do. I'm going to take you home. Then I'm going to take *that*"—Fay pointed to the Middleton Stone—"to the police."

"Fine." Pru was too tired to argue. It had been an impossible day, and the police station would be the safest place for the Middleton Stone, anyway. Thor was there. "Fay? I know I said this before, but thank you. Really."

"You don't need to thank me, Pru. I'm just glad that everything worked out for the best."

✧

Pru and Fay rode the rest of the way to Pru's house in a comfortable silence. The silence, and the comfort, ended abruptly when Pru arrived home to her mother.

Pru's emotions were a jumble as she followed her mother into the living room, working on a slightly modified version of the story she'd told Fay: She'd been in town when she saw someone suspicious. She'd heard about the robbery on the news, and decided to follow the suspicious man to the cemetery. There she'd found the Middleton Stone.

She was about to gloss over her escape when her mother brought her hand down hard on the sofa cushion.

"Pru, are you insane?" Pru flinched. "You followed a strange man to the cemetery? Do you have any idea what could have happened to you?"

"I'm fine, Mom."

"You're not fine, Pru! You haven't been since . . ." Pru's mother stopped and took a deep breath. She reached out and put her hand over Pru's, but Pru pulled away.

"Pru," her mother said as she tried to control her breathing, "I know you're angry. I don't understand why you're angry at me, but if that's what you need to feel right now, that's fine. But you have to understand, I'm just trying to keep you safe."

That was too much.

Pru stood up. She imagined that her eyes were as fierce as any thunder god's eyes had ever been.

"Yeah? Well, you're not doing a very good job of it, are you?"

She stormed up to her room.

☆

Pru tossed and turned all that night, trapped in a nightmare of giants and thieves and houses too small to contain all the lies that dwelt within.

In her nightmare, Pru heard her mother's voice calling her home as she ran through a dead forest beneath burned skies. Fox-headed monsters in gray coats chased her and promised to be her friend, even as they

182

reached out to drag her back to their crooked home where she'd never see the sun again. All the while, Pru screamed "How could you?" at the monsters over and over again. Deep down, though, she knew the answer. She'd known for a long time now. Because this was what adults did.

They lied.

Pru scrambled out of bed eager to escape her dream and more eager to act. Fortunately, the morning brought clarity. She'd made a mistake. She never should have put Fay in danger by letting her take the Middleton Stone. Fay had no idea what she was getting into. Pru should have insisted on bringing it to Thor herself.

Hopefully, Fay had delivered the stone to the police station and Thor being there had been enough to keep Loki away. The world hadn't ended yet, anyway. Pru took that as a good sign.

Still, something had to be done about Loki. Pru couldn't stand the thought of him lurking around town. Her only choice was to go to Winterhaven House, expose Loki to Odin, and hope that Odin would punish the liar.

A lot.

Pru dressed and crept down the stairs of her house. She paused as she passed the telephone. She desperately wanted to call ABE. Her hand hovered over the phone. She already felt relieved knowing she could confide in him again. She'd even find his squeaky voice reassuring. But that thought reminded her of how mean she'd been to him the day before. He probably wouldn't want to talk to her.

And even if he did, it occurred to her that she didn't know his number. She also didn't know where ABE lived. She'd never asked. She'd never taken the time to learn much about him at all, actually.

If she were ABE, she wouldn't want to talk to her, either.

Turning from the phone, Pru slipped into the kitchen and scrawled a note to leave for her mom on the refrigerator. She explained that she wanted to get an early start for the first day of the Explorers' Fair. As quietly as possible, she turned the front doorknob, shut the door behind her, and slipped away.

Pru had been to the Explorers' Fair before, of course. Pretty much everyone in town went every year, even if they didn't like Vikings. This year felt different, though. She maneuvered through the growing crowd in a state of ever-increasing anxiety. While some of the fairgoers' outfits were obviously costumes, with their plastic horns and braided wigs, others were frighteningly realistic. People who she should have easily recognized as neighbors took on a more sinister appearance as they brandished costume weaponry and fierce looks.

Were they people at a fair or other characters from Norse mythology poised to strike?

Pru studied each face carefully, desperate to determine whether it was someone she recognized from town. And she kept a sharp eye out for ABE, hoping that maybe he'd appear in the crowd. He never did.

Pru's first thought had been to go immediately to the mansion and try to find Odin. But as she made her way through the crowd, Pru saw the booth for the Earth Center and changed course toward it.

"Have you seen Fay?" she asked one of the adult volunteers she recognized. She thought his name might be Bob.

Maybe-Bob turned with a distracted look from the pyramid of aluminum cans he was building. "Who? Fay? No . . . no, I can't say I have."

Pru sped off, trying to ignore that first, feather touch of actual fear. She soon encountered one more distraction on her path to Winterhaven House.

"Roger!" she exclaimed, recognizing her dad's old partner as she neared the stone mansion.

"Hey, kiddo. You're up early. Where's your mom?"

"She's still sleeping. It's Saturday, you know?" While Roger chuckled, Pru took in his pressed pants, jacket, and tie. It could only mean one thing. "You're all dressed up—and not like a Viking. Are you on duty?"

"Afraid so. No rest for the weary. Did you hear?

Someone stole some old stone out of the Grimnir Collection. Probably a crazy rock collector, or something."

"I heard." Pru tried to sound casual as fear slowly tightened its fist on her insides. "But I also thought I heard someone found the stone and returned it."

"Returned it? I don't think so. I'd be the first to know. Where did you hear that?"

"Uh, nowhere," Pru said. "I mean, I must have heard wrong. Look, I've got to go. Sorry!"

Pru took off once more. Fear had her completely in its grip now. What had happened to Fay? Why hadn't she returned the stone? Had Loki caught her before she made it to the police station?

Lost in thought, Pru ran right into another fairgoer—a sturdy one, too, judging by the way Pru rebounded. She looked up, ready to let the offender have it, but she held her tongue when recognition hit. It was Hilde, from Winterhaven House!

She wore a rough leather tunic and a long blue cloak that nearly hid the sword that hung at her side. Another year, Pru would have assumed Hilde was dressed for the fair. Now, Pru suspected that the woman was dressed in her usual way. If Hilde worked for Old Man Grimnir, there was a good chance Hilde was a Mythic, too.

"Are you going somewhere?" Pru asked, noticing a leather pack slung over Hilde's shoulder.

"I am," Hilde said, looking down at Pru without surprise. "Mr. Grimnir has already left. The event he came to witness has happened, as it was always going to."

"But you can't go. And you have to get Odin back!" Pru bit her lower lip. She'd never outed a Viking god in public before and wasn't quite sure of the proper way to go about it, but this was important. "Loki is here. He's on Midgard! He defied Odin. And I think he might have hurt a friend of mine—"

The words spilled out of Pru's mouth with increasing speed. She took a deep breath, trying to force herself to slow down. Instead, Hilde stopped her altogether.

"Be at ease. You have nothing to fear from Loki, child. He has left this place. The giants have gone with him. Odin told me."

Pru blinked, taken aback.

"He has? They did?" That was good news, wasn't it? So why did Pru still feel so worried? "But what about my friend?"

"You will discover the truth about your friend soon. When you do discover the truth, try not to be too hard on yourself. Loki has fooled us all at one time or another." With that, Hilde took a step back as two Viking-clad fairgoers walked between her and Pru. When the fairgoers had passed, Hilde had vanished.

Pru spun in a slow circle, not sure what to do next. Around her, the grounds filled as more people joined the festivities. Noise, bustle, guilt, worry—and an absurd number of silly Viking hats with horns—made it impossible for Pru to think. She fled to the edge of the estate grounds, to the border of the woods, where she collapsed against a tree and slid down into a sitting position with her forehead pressed against her knees. One question rose above the clamor in her head.

Where was Fay?

Hilde had said Pru would find out soon and that she shouldn't blame herself . . . But if something terrible had happened to Fay, then who else was to blame?

As upsetting as that thought was, there was something else. Pru was missing something. She could feel it. Something didn't make sense.

"There's something wrong, and I just can't see it," Pru said aloud. She didn't expect a response. She got one anyway.

"Well," a voice replied from above, "don't go blaming me if something's wrong. *You* didn't listen to me. *I* said you were in terrible danger. *I* tried to warn you. But does anyone ever want to listen to what *I* have to say? Ha!"

Surprise lifted Pru to her feet and spun her around, already sure of what—or who—she'd see above. Sure enough, a small gray squirrel with a droopy tail lay sprawled across a branch overhead.

"You! You're Ratatosk, right?"

"No," the squirrel said, "I'm the *other* talking squirrel."

He was clearly in a mood.

Unfortunately, so was Pru.

"You know what? I don't have time for this. I have one friend missing, one friend mad at me because I was mean to him, and one friend who isn't my friend at all. He's just a big, fat liar. Now I've got to figure out what to do about it all, so why don't *you* go gather some acorns or something." She turned her back on the squirrel.

"Go gather some acorns? *Go gather some acorns?* You can't talk to me like that. I'm Ratatosk, messenger to the gods!"

"More like messenger to some overgrown lizard and birdbrain," Pru said, looking over her shoulder and remembering what she'd read about how Ratatosk delivered messages between a dragon and an eagle.

"How dare you?" Ratatosk's tail poofed to an alarming degree. "You mewling ingrate! You serpent-tongued half troll! You fish-bellied shortwit!"

"Hey!" Pru interrupted, spinning around. "I'm not short!"

Ratatosk rolled his eyes, a gesture that Pru found even more insulting than usual when performed by a squirrel.

"No, no, no," he chattered in a patronizing voice.

"It's no fun at all insulting you if you don't know what I'm saying. I didn't call you short."

"Oh. Okay, then . . ."

"I called you an idiot."

"Hey!" All the insults Pru had heard (and given) in the schoolyard scrolled through her mind as she scrambled for a response. "Yeah, well, you're so stupid, you could get hit by a parked car."

As soon as the words were out of her mouth, Pru realized she'd crossed a line. Who knew how many of Ratatosk's friends and relatives had found themselves on the wrong end of a speeding sedan? Ratatosk's eyes widened and he clutched his tail.

"Okay, look, I'm sorry." Pru slumped against another nearby tree as Ratatosk stared at her in horror. "I'm under a lot of pressure. Loki made a fool out of me and now I don't know what to do."

Ratatosk snorted, but he also released his tail. In a somewhat sympathetic voice, he said, "Don't feel bad. Loki fools everyone, sooner or later—usually more than once, yes, and often before breakfast."

Ratatosk sounded like he was speaking from experience. Pru thought back to what else she'd read about the squirrel at Winterhaven House. The sign had said that Ratatosk often knew more about the gods' comings and goings than even they suspected.

"Has Loki ever fooled you?" she asked, following a hunch.

Ratatosk began to tug on his tail again. The gesture reminded Pru of ABE running his hands through his hair. "Maybe."

"It was you, wasn't it?" Pru leaned forward. "I wondered how Loki found the stone here in our town. I mean, nobody comes to Middleton. You told him it was here, didn't you? Because you didn't have to *find* it. I bet you *saw* Odin hide the rune stone here, all those years ago."

"I am outraged by your accusation!" Ratatosk exclaimed. "Incensed. Infuriated! How dare you suggest I would spy on the Allfather? I never would, no, no, no!" Then, sounding slightly less outraged, he added, "It's not my fault I *accidentally* saw him hide it one day, while minding my own business in the Allfather's general vicinity."

"And did you tell Loki?"

From the way Ratatosk settled back on his haunches and looked away, Pru suspected that if squirrels could blush, Ratatosk would be bright red.

"Well, technically, I suppose I did. But just because Loki asked nicely. It only took him a few thousand years to think of me. But that's the problem, isn't it? No one *ever* thinks of talking to me. It's always, 'Ratatosk, go

191

tell that carrion-eating stinkfart *this*,' or, 'Ratatosk, go tell that weak-winged crow *that*.' A lifetime of carrying other people's nasty little words, and no one asking to hear mine."

"That does sound pretty lousy," Pru admitted. She began to understand why Ratatosk used so many words when he *did* get a chance to talk.

"Then Loki came along and he was nice. Kind. Considerate. He told me that all those insults I had to carry did nothing but build walls, and if there was one thing he understood, it was the importance of *not* building walls. He said that if I helped him find the Eye of Odin, we'd be friends and he'd change things so that I never had to carry another insult again. But as soon as he knew where the rune stone was, he didn't have time to listen to me anymore."

"Wait," Pru said, frowning. "Loki said that about not building walls?"

"Yes. Why?"

"It's nothing. I'm sure it's nothing. It's just, I have a friend who says the same thing. She's pretty much my only friend at this point."

My closest friend.

Pru's eyes widened in horror and Ratatosk took a step back, scanning for a predator.

"What is it?" he asked.

"Oh no." Blood rushed to Pru's head. It carried with it a tide of memories. Words and images flooded her brain.

Building walls. She remembered "The Story of Loki and the Building of Asgard's Wall." In it, Loki was forced to stop the building of the wall around Asgard. Fay's voice reverberated through Pru's mind.

"And if there's one thing I understand, it's the importance of not building walls."

Other memories rushed in then, wave after wave of recollection. The story had also said that Loki wasn't actually a Norse god. It said he lived among them, though, and that the other gods had always been suspicious of him, even as a youth. Fay's voice once again echoed in Pru's head.

"But where I grew up, I was very different from those around me. Some things that were very easy for my peers were difficult for me."

"No!" Pru repeated. It wasn't true. Fay couldn't be Loki. Loki was a man!

Except when he wasn't.

One last memory from the story surfaced. In it, Loki had changed into a mare, a *female* horse, to distract the builder's stallion. Loki had even given birth to an eight-legged foal while in that form, which he'd given to Odin as a gift.

"Though motherhood came to me unexpectedly, and it saddens me to say that I gave my child to someone else to raise shortly after his birth."

The tide of memories receded and left Pru with the truth.

She'd been wrong. She'd been so wrong.

"It wasn't ABE or Mister Fox," Pru said to Ratatosk. "It never was." She covered her face with her hands. "The whole time, it was Fay."

A shadow stretched out from the woods as someone approached Pru from behind. She didn't bother to look up. She knew instantly to whom the shadow belonged. This time, for the first time, his appearance didn't startle her at all.

CHAPTER 20

"I'M GLAD YOU TWO SORTED THAT OUT, BECAUSE WE have work to do," Mister Fox said, leaving the cover of the trees and walking up to Pru.

"Stay away from me," Pru said, taking a step back.

"What's wrong?" A gust of wind swirled the coat around the detective's feet as he came to a stop, frowning. "You know I'm not Loki. I just heard you say it."

"So you didn't lie to me about being an evil being from another world who was going to someday start a war that kills pretty much everyone. So what?" Pru folded her arms across her chest. "You still yelled at me."

"Pru, listen to me, we don't have time for hurt feelings. Something's happened."

Pru's arms remained folded as she remembered the look of rage she'd seen on Mister Fox's face when he'd found her in the Henhouse. She took another step back.

"Fine," Mister Fox grumbled, pinching the bridge of his nose between his thumb and forefinger. "Right. We'll make time. Okay, look, Pru, I'm sorry. This is something you won't hear me say very often . . . but I made a mistake. I didn't think I was yelling at you. I thought I was yelling at Loki."

"What?" The tension left Pru's arms and they dropped to her sides.

Mister Fox released his nose and looked at Pru. "Once you and ABE discovered the true power of the Eye of Odin and I understood the danger it presented, I decided the Middleton Stone would be safest with me. So I took the stone and brought it to the Henhouse. No one's supposed to be able to get in there without my knowing. When I arrived home and discovered someone there, I assumed the only person who could have possibly broken into the Henhouse was Loki. Do you understand now? Loki fooled me, too."

"Wait. How could you think I was Loki? I never even got a chance to tell you Loki was mixed up in things."

"No offense to your squirrel friend, but your town is being invaded by beings from Norse mythology. Anytime there's trouble involving Norse mythology, you can pretty much expect Loki to be part of it. He's the well-established troublemaker of the group."

"But if you knew Loki was involved, how come you didn't tell me and ABE?"

"You already know why. You're no good to me if you believe everything you're told. You needed to keep an open mind and discover your own answers. Which, obviously, you did." Mister Fox's nose twitched. "Out of curiosity, how *did* you figure out Loki was involved?"

"Thor told me."

At Mister Fox's prompting, she explained her discovery of the imprisoned thunder god. As she spoke, she reviewed her experience in the Henhouse in her mind. Seen through the lens of this new information, Mister Fox's reaction to finding her in the Henhouse did make sense.

"And you're sure Thor won't help?" Mister Fox asked when Pru had finished.

"Pretty sure, yeah. He won't disobey his dad again. He said he's going to stay in jail until his dad lets him go. Then he's going back to Asgard."

"That's a shame. We could have used him. As I was saying, we have a problem."

"I know."

"You do?" Mister Fox sounded surprised.

"Obviously." Pru braced herself for Mister Fox's reaction. "I gave Loki the Middleton Stone."

"That? That wasn't your fault. Loki is called the Lord of Lies for a reason. Of course he fooled you. He even fooled me, and *that's* saying something."

"Someone's a little sure of himself," Pru said. Despite her teasing, though, she could feel a wave of relief passing through her at the realization that Mister Fox was once more an ally. Irritating as he could be, he was also clever (not that she'd admit it to him). He could fix this! Her relief faltered a bit, though, as she saw the look of irritation on Mister Fox's face.

"The point is, your mistake is not the problem. The problem is ABE. He's missing. I think Loki took him."

"What? Why would Loki take—" Pru cut herself off as the last clue fell into place. "Of course. ABE figured it out."

"What did ABE figure out?" Mister Fox peered at Pru. "That Fay was Loki? How do you know that?"

Pru reached for a nearby branch. Breaking off a stick, she used it to begin scratching letters in the dirt. "I'm an idiot! I should have seen it right away. I found these words in ABE's notebook," she explained as she scrawled them out: I AM OFTEN LYING.

"I was so stupid! I thought ABE was confessing to being Loki. That's why I went to the Henhouse in the first place. But it wasn't a confession! The answer was right in front of me. There were other words above those. They were crossed out, though, so I didn't look at them hard."

Now, however, Pru reversed ABE's process. She crossed out one letter of his so-called confession at a time and rewrote the letters in a new arrangement: FAY LONINGTIME.

"She told us." The stick dropped from Pru's hand as she stared down at Fay's name. "She told us the very first day we met her that there were secret messages in her name. She—he—was taunting us the whole time. ABE's crazy for words and riddles. Plus, he's read all the Norse myths. He found this secret message in Fay's name and figured out the lying was a reference to Loki. And he figured it out *at* the Earth Center. He's way too honest. It would have shown all over his face."

Mister Fox studied the words in the dirt. "And Loki knew he'd been caught, so he took ABE to keep him from talking," he said. "You're right. That has Loki written all over it. Not literally, of course, but almost. Look. There's another possible arrangement."

Bending to retrieve Pru's stick, he rearranged the letters once more, this time spelling out FOALING ENMITY.

"That's Loki, to be sure," he said. "Foaling, of course, means giving birth to a baby horse. And enmity means hatred. Who but Loki has reason to hate giving birth to a baby horse?"

"What are we going to do?" Pru drove her foot into the ground and began grinding out the letters, trying to erase every last trace of Loki's tricks and her stupidity. "What if ABE's . . ."

"ABE's alive," Mister Fox assured her. "The Henhouse places certain enchantments on anyone who enters it. I'd know if ABE were hurt, or worse. He's alive. I just don't know where. The good news is, he's not on Earth."

"How is *that* good news?"

"Because it means Loki is either on Asgard or Niflheim, and time passes differently on Worlds of Myth. We have time to figure out where Loki's gone, and where he's taken ABE."

"Loki must be going after the Eye," Pru said.

"Agreed. Unfortunately, both Asgard and Niflheim are big places. Since we don't know where the Eye is, we don't know where to start looking."

In the near silence that followed Mister Fox's statement, Pru heard a small sound. Or, rather, the sound of someone small, clearing his throat.

"Ratatosk!" Pru felt a thrill of understanding and hope. "You know, don't you? You know where Odin hid the Eye. You read what was on the stone, didn't you?"

"Well, maybe a little," Ratatosk admitted. "But you can't tell Odin. He would think I was being nosy, and he doesn't like that. I wasn't, of course!"

"Of course not," Pru agreed. "You were minding your own business . . . in the general vicinity of the rune stone."

"Exactly!"

"So where is it?" Mister Fox asked.

"It's in the nest of that lice-ridden eagle perched atop Yggdrasil. Otherwise, I'd go get the Eye myself, just to hide it from Loki again. But that bird is bad news."

"Okay," Mister Fox said. "I can work with that. The Henhouse can get us to Asgard and close enough to Yggdrasil to find Loki and ABE."

Mister Fox's gaze traveled from Ratatosk to Pru. His expression darkened.

"After that, Pru, it's going to be up to you to save ABE."

"What do you mean? We'll save him together."

"I can't."

"Of course you can. The Henhouse can take us to Asgard. You said so. Then we'll find ABE and stop Loki." Pru couldn't understand why Mister Fox was suddenly being so dense.

Mister Fox drew his hand across his face, pulling at his chin.

"Pru, I *can't*."

"Stop saying that!" Pru's hair spun in the air as she shook her head back and forth. "What does that even mean? Why can't you?"

"Because of what you just said. I'm too sure of myself."

"That? You're mad because I said *that*? I'm sorry, okay? I take it back."

"You can't take it back, Pru, because you're right. I am too sure of myself. That's the problem. It all comes back to belief and the certainty it breeds. Like I told you that day in the Henhouse, only those people who are unsure of what they believe are able to experience magic. That means that only people who are unsure of what they believe are able to travel to Worlds of Myth."

"I get it. So what?"

"So here's what you have to understand. Nowadays, those people are all children. All of them. Children are like the early people who discovered the Worlds of Myth in the first place. They're still new to the world. They're not so sure of things."

The detective removed his hat and massaged the bridge of his long nose. Pru thought he looked tired. He'd never looked tired to her before.

"Things change as you get older," he said. "This is going to be hard for you to understand, but as we age we accumulate experiences, a terrible wealth of experiences. Those experiences teach us who we are. That's the trade-off. As you grow up, you trade possibility for certainty. I'm sure of myself. I *know* who I am. I know what I think and what I'm capable of. Mind you, I'm capable of some pretty amazing things. But traveling to Asgard or any World of Myth isn't one of those things, not anymore. I've lived too long in the world."

"But you *can* experience magic," Pru argued. "I've seen it. You talk to squirrels. You fight giants."

"You're right. I spent most of my childhood traveling in the Henhouse through Worlds of Myth, and because of that I'm still able to do some things that other adults can't. If something comes into this world, I can see it, usually. More and more, though, I need help. My looking glass gives me focus, and so does seeing through the eyes of young Fibbers. The older I get, the more I miss. Every year, every day, the magic slips further and further away."

The detective paused to look off into the distance.

"Sometimes I'm afraid that I'll return to the Henhouse one day and she just won't be there anymore. Or, worse, she'll be there, but I won't be able to see her." He returned his gaze to Pru. "So, yes, I still get to have *some* fun. But only here in this world."

Pru put a hand on her forehead as the reality of Mister Fox's words sank in. A vein beneath her skin pulsed, rhythmic, like the ticking of a clock. *Ba-boom, ba-boom.*

"And you'd let me go . . . ?" she whispered.

Ba-boom. Tick. Tock.

What time is it, Mister Fox?

"Yes," the detective said. "If anyone is going to go save ABE, it's going to have to be you."

Midnight.

CHAPTER
21

MYSTERY AND ADVENTURE WERE ONE THING. TRAV-
eling between worlds that a week ago Pru hadn't even
known existed was something else altogether. Pru
wanted ABE to be safe. But hadn't her father wanted
to keep people safe? And hadn't that turned out to be
a deadly mistake?

Ratatosk had agreed to travel to Asgard ahead of
Pru to do some scouting and then to meet her when
she arrived. The promise of the squirrel's company
was briefly reassuring. Pru's resolve to go on alone to
Asgard lasted until she and Mister Fox reached the
edge of the cemetery. Then it fled, and so did she.

Pru was kneeling at the foot of her father's grave
when Mister Fox caught up to her. She didn't look up

as she heard him approach. She just traced the letters, written in stone, in front of her. *Beloved Father.*

"You can't make me go," she said as the detective came to a stop.

"No, I can't."

"So why are you even here?" Pru said, wiping a sleeve across her face.

Mister Fox waited. He stood behind her dad's headstone, appearing to rise up behind it, stone-faced and grave.

"Say something!" Pru stood and faced the detective. "You're useless! You're not even trying to help me! You don't care!"

Silence in the graveyard.

"It's not supposed to be like this!" Pru raged.

"Like what, Pru?"

"You're not supposed to leave!"

The words tore up through Pru from someplace deep inside her. They were alive and they were angry, and they came up all on their own.

"You're the grown-up! You're supposed to stay! You're supposed to keep me safe." Pru gasped for air as the storm that had been coming for such a long time finally broke. "That's all you grown-ups ever talk about, right? *Keeping kids safe.* But it's such a lie. You're all such liars! You leave when we need you and *nothing is safe!*"

"And there it is," Mister Fox said, his voice soft, a whisper among the dead. "The greatest lie of them all. The worst lie of them all, and the one we tell most often to ourselves and to our children—that the world is safe, or that it can be made so."

"So you admit it! You admit you're all liars!"

"Do I admit I'm a liar? I admit to having a complicated relationship with the truth, on occasion," the detective said with a sly smile, which might have also been a little sad. "But in this instance I think you'll find me innocent. I never told you the world was safe. But I'm sure others have. And it's a wonderful lie, isn't it? A beautiful fiction."

"Not when you see through it," Pru spat.

"No. No, not when you see through it. Still, in my experience, some people live their whole lives and never have to confront this particular lie. They stay safe, and so do the people they love. But you're right. Other people learn the truth, and some of them learn it at far too young an age."

"So what are those people supposed to even do?" she said. The words came from the empty place inside Pru.

"I don't know the answer to that question," Mister Fox said. He took a deep breath. "Not for sure. But I'll tell you what I think. I think those people find a way through the woods. Different people take different

207

paths, but most of them find a way, sooner or later. Because, in the end, I think it all comes back to those stories about the things that children find in the woods."

"Wolves. Witches. Giants," Pru said, remembering her first real conversation with the man in gray, on a day that had vibrated with fear but also newness and the excitement of things not-yet-discovered.

Mister Fox continued. "You know, there are whole volumes of stories about the terrible things that children can find in the woods. Most people see those stories as warnings to stay away, to stay safe. I don't. Because if you think about it, all those stories that are supposedly meant to keep children out of the woods tell them something else, too. They tell them that's where the magic is."

As Mister Fox spoke, a small crack appeared in the clouds overhead. The thinnest ray of sun shone through, the first in what felt like forever, almost as if it had been prearranged.

"So you see," Mister Fox said, "I don't think those stories are a warning at all. I think they're a message. They tell you that you can't have magic without monsters. Now, some people spend their whole lives trying to hide from the monsters because they can make the world a frightening place. And the world *can* be frightening. It can be terrifying. That's the truth. But that's not the *entire* truth. There's a difference. There are whole worlds of difference between things that are true and the entire truth.

"The entire truth is that *anything* is possible, Pru, not just the awful things. Not just the monsters. There's magic out there, too, in the woods, in the world. Talking squirrels. Brave companions. Traveling houses. There's so much to see and explore, if only we're open to it. If only we're willing to risk being unsafe and unsure, at least on occasion."

Adjusting the brim of his hat, Mister Fox looked Pru directly in the eye.

"I'll never tell you that there aren't monsters out there. And I can't promise you'll always be safe from them. This is what I can tell you, Pru. My truth. There are things out there in the world that are worth braving the monsters for."

Listening, Pru felt herself fill with something new, something that hadn't been there before. It felt something like hope, but one fact remained.

"I'm scared."

"Of course you are. I was when I was your age and I faced a similar situation."

"You faced giants?"

"No. But I faced a witch, remember? And even though I was frightened at first, that encounter set me on a path of adventure," Mister Fox said, with a twitching nose. "I'm still on that path, really. But you've heard my story. Now it's time for you and your story. And being scared is a good way to start a story. It's smart to be scared. Just don't make the mistake that so many people make. Don't *just* be scared. Because scared is such a little thing, when you look at it. I mean, when you really look at it, it's tiny. And you, you're so much bigger."

Pru snorted at that, unaccustomed as she was to being called big.

"Well, not literally, of course," Mister Fox corrected. "I mean, physically speaking, you're a bit small for your age."

Inside her sneaker, Pru flexed the toes of her kicking foot.

"But that's the thing about being a kid, isn't it? Kids are the Henhouse. Deceptively small on the outside, and so full of possibility on the inside. That's why you can do things I can't. Because you're made of possibility. It's not a choice or a state of mind. It's who you are. You can do anything. Giants? Giants should flee in terror from people who are a bit small for their age."

Pru hesitated. She'd been afraid for such a long time. It was hard to let go. "What will happen if I don't go? Will ABE be okay?"

Mister Fox looked off into the distance again.

"Sure he will," he said, after considering the question for a moment. "ABE's a smart kid. He'll be fine. Everything will work out for the best."

Pru considered that.

"I don't believe you," she said finally.

"No. I don't suppose you do."

In that moment, Pru understood why Mister Fox always smiled with that lopsided grin of his. Even as joy and delight lifted one side of his mouth, grief and loss weighed down the other.

"So what do I do first?" she asked. "What happens now?"

"Now? Isn't it obvious? Now, Prudence Potts, now you have an adventure."

CHAPTER 22

PRU AND MISTER FOX RETURNED TO THE HENHOUSE to find the doors open and waiting. Inside, Mister Fox led Pru to a new room filled with maps, where he proceeded to select, unroll, and promptly discard a number of parchments before finally uncovering the one he wanted.

Pru nearly jumped out of her skin when a pair of floating hands appeared to take the selected map from Mister Fox, who seemed not at all surprised by the development.

"What was that?" Pru demanded.

"That was one of the *domovye*. You *really* ought to pay attention. They're how I communicate with the Henhouse. I would have introduced you, but they're still a little upset with you for trying to set fire to the place."

With a twinge of guilt, Pru recalled knocking down the oil lamps. She also recalled the noise that had drawn her into the Henhouse the day before and wondered if the *domovye* had been responsible for that.

Not long after the spirit departed, the Henhouse lurched the way a person might when getting up for a stretch after a long sit. The sound of creaking wood and rustling feathers once more filled the air—only this time it came from all around Pru. Again, Mister Fox gave no evidence of being surprised.

The rustling sound was followed by the unmistakable sensation of traveling up, like being in an elevator. Pru grabbed a nearby table and held on for her life. "What's happening? Are we *flying*?"

"That's not quite the word I'd use."

The Henhouse's ascent slowed, and for one breathless moment it seemed to hang in the air. Then Pru experienced the equally unmistakable but far more alarming sensation of falling, like she imagined it would feel to be in an elevator plunging downward so fast that you *just know* that you're about to get squashed.

"We're falling!" Pru shouted when she was able to catch her breath.

"Now *that's* the exact word I'd use," Mister Fox said, laughing.

This wasn't an elevator ride for him—it was a roller coaster.

Pru barely had time to imagine what life as a pancake might be like before the Henhouse's downward motion came to a bouncy but otherwise not-flattening stop.

"What just happened?" Pru said between gasps. "That was unbelievable!"

"That? That was nothing. You want to see unbelievable?" He led Pru back to the front doors and opened them. "*This* is unbelievable."

The doors opened onto a world that was new. Pru exited the Henhouse and looked out on Asgard. She saw grass so green and a sky so blue and wide and open that it almost hurt to look at them. It made her feel small and big all at the same time. The horizon lay infinitely far away, across an endless plain, and yet Pru felt she could reach out and touch it with her finger, the way kids in a schoolyard will eclipse the sun with their thumb and seem to know what it's like to be able to touch the stars.

"What do you see?" Mister Fox asked.

Pru turned around to find the detective shrouded in the shadows of the Henhouse, a few steps behind her. The light from Asgard didn't touch him.

"You can't see it, can you?"

"Not from here, no." Mister Fox's face was unreadable. "If I go upstairs to the round window you saw on your first visit, then I can see. That glass is enchanted like my looking glass. But from here, all I see is the graveyard, always and only the graveyard. So tell me, what's out there?"

"A big open plain, covered in grass." Pru walked to the edge of the small porch and looked around the corner. "And over there, on the left, there's a mountain in the distance. It's a really big one. It goes right up into the clouds."

She squinted, her eyes still adjusting to the light.

"No, wait. I don't think it is a mountain, actually. It's . . ." She brought a hand up to shield her eyes and get a better look. "No way."

"What is it?"

"It's . . . it's an upside-down tree," Pru said. "But that's impossible. The trunk is coming down from the clouds, and the branches are all spread out into the ground. It's *huge*. Also, did I mention? It's upside down. How does a tree even get to be that big? *And upside down*."

"That's Yggdrasil, the giant ash tree that has one root in each of the three worlds of Norse mythology. You're seeing the root that goes into Asgard. Loki will be somewhere there, looking for the Eye of Odin. ABE will be there, too."

"But it's so far away, and Loki has a whole day's head start."

"You're still thinking in terms of your world. Worlds of Myth are immortal realms. Time and distance work differently here. We got here sooner than you think, and the distance is less than you think. Now, is there any sign of Ratatosk?"

"No," Pru answered, scanning the horizon again.

"You'll have to start without him. Events will move more quickly now that we're here in Asgard. Take this." Mister Fox reached into his coat pocket and removed his looking glass. "It allows me to track Mythics. As they move through Earth, their passing creates a disturbance in the air like the sheen of oil in water. The looking glass magnifies the effect and makes it easier to see. The same principle will work in reverse here. With this, you'll be able to track ABE's movements across Asgard."

Pru considered the vast distance before her. It seemed so far to go.

"What if I'm not good enough?" she asked. Then, before Mister Fox could argue, she added, "No, really. I mean, ABE was better. Don't *ever* tell him I said that. But he figured out who Fay was before I did. He saw the message in her name first."

After a moment's hesitation, Mister Fox stepped out onto the porch. The light of Asgard's sun still didn't touch him. In fact, he appeared more gray than usual. Only his eyes stood out, blue and clear.

"And is that how you discovered the truth about Fay?" Mister Fox asked, his nose twitching.

"Well, no. I sort of figured it out from something Ratatosk said about Loki that reminded me of Fay."

"I thought as much. Listen, Pru. ABE is brilliant. He is. But the thing about ABE is that he's so . . . honest. That's what makes him ABE. And he's so honest himself, he sees the world honestly. He sees the truth of things."

Pru hadn't thought of it like that, but it made sense.

"But as ABE sees truth, Pru, you see possibilities. You make connections and put pieces together. Where ABE sees things how they are, you see things how they could be. And that's what all the very best detectives do."

Pru straightened her shoulders and drew in her breath. "Thanks . . . really. Okay. Right. I can do this. I can chase down Loki and get ABE back from a small army of frost giants. Because I see things how they could be. And because I've got a magnifying glass. But, you know, it's also a mirror, so no sweat."

Pru's shoulders drooped as, despite her best efforts to stay positive, the reality of what she was about to try pressed in. "Seriously. What am I supposed to do, ask Loki and the giants nicely to give me ABE back?"

"You, ask nicely? Now *that's* something I'd like to see."

"That's not funny." But it was, kind of, and Pru felt a little better.

"Pru, you've got more than the looking glass at your disposal. Think about it. On Earth, Mythics pass unnoticed because they're from a different world. What do you think that means for you, a mortal, here on Asgard?"

"I'll be invisible!" Pru exclaimed as understanding struck. "Is that right? That is so cool."

"Not quite invisible, no. But you'll be unnoticeable. It's not just a matter of sight. Do you know the saying 'Out of sight, out of mind'? That's almost how it works here: Out of mind, out of sight. Mythics won't see you here because they don't have you in their thoughts. They won't be able to focus on you visually or mentally."

"Like my mom when I tried to show her your invitation, or Sergeant Mahoney with Thor."

"Exactly. Just don't do anything to call attention to yourself and you'll be able to slip in, find ABE, and slip out."

"But what about the Eye of Odin?"

"One thing at a time. Get in, get ABE, get out. Got it?"

Pru nodded.

"Good. Off you go, then. Have fun and try not to get stepped on."

Pru decided she would take the high road and not stick her tongue out. Then she stuck it out anyway, quickly, and turned to take her first steps into a new world.

☆

Time and distance blurred as Pru ran across the Asgardian plain. No matter how far or fast she went, she didn't tire. The air filled her lungs and nourished her. The grass beneath her feet did more than cushion her steps, it compelled them and drove her on. She felt like she could run forever.

Pru intercepted ABE's trail soon enough—it appeared just like Mister Fox had said it would, a glow in the air not unlike the sheen of oil on water. It was the same effect Pru had seen at the Fort of the Fallen in the moments after the giant's disappearance. Sure enough, it led right to Yggdrasil.

The giant tree grew larger as Pru drew closer. Far overhead, the single root split again and again. As it neared the ground, it created a forest of smaller roots, each as large as any tree on Earth. When Pru arrived at the outer edge of that forest of roots, she saw that it extended as far as she could see in either direction. Drawing a deep breath, she stepped inside.

Though no leaves graced the tops of the treelike growths all around her, the woodland through which Pru moved swarmed with greenery and life. Moss covered stones, and the green shoots of shaded plants were everywhere. They filled the air with a pleasant, emerald tint as all manner of animals scampered about. Pru saw deer and birds. Once, she spotted a fox, which she took as a good omen. She did not see any squirrels, although she kept her eyes (and ears) open for one in particular.

A few steps into the growth, Pru remembered to check the fox-head looking glass once more. The light shimmering through the glass was getting brighter. She seemed to be getting close.

At a rustling in the undergrowth, Pru halted. Her first thought was that Ratatosk might have found her. But whatever was causing the rustling was too big to be a squirrel. It was also getting closer. Pru found a particularly thick root behind which she could hide. She crouched and willed herself to be unnoticeable.

A figure emerged from the greenery, slightly taller than Pru, with a mess of blond hair and no freckles at all, which Pru hardly noticed as a surge of relief swept through her.

"ABE!" She leapt forward and grabbed ABE in a hug.

"Pru? Is that really you?" It was hard to tell what startled ABE more, Pru's appearance or the fact that she was hugging him.

"It's me," she said, releasing him and stepping back.

"But . . . I . . . What are you doing here?"

"I came to save you. Not like you needed it, though. How in the world—in *any* world—did you get away?"

"It was the squirrel," ABE said, still sounding stunned.

"Ratatosk? You saw him?" Pru looked around. "Where is he?"

"He stayed behind to keep an eye on Loki and the giants. Loki!" ABE grabbed Pru's sleeve. "Pru, Fay was Loki from the stories. The trickster. Remember? I figured it out from her name—his name. Anyway, he was in charge of the giants all along. He found out the Eye of Odin was at the top of Yggdrasil. He must have gotten the Middleton Stone somehow."

"Yeah," Pru said, coughing into her hand. "Somehow. But that's not important right now. You were telling me how you got away."

"Well, Ratatosk found me and he chewed through the ropes holding me. Then I just snuck off. It was the weirdest thing, actually. As soon as we got to Asgard, it was almost like Loki and the giants forgot all about me. They dragged me along, but half the time it was like they didn't even remember I was there."

"That makes sense, actually," Pru said. She explained how she and ABE were unnoticeable on Asgard.

"That explains a lot. But what about you? How did you get here?"

"Mister Fox brought me in the Henhouse."

"That's great! Where is he? Can he take us home?"

"He's back that way." Pru gestured. "We *could* go back, but . . ."

"But what? What else would we do?"

"ABE, I found Thor. I talked to him. He told me all about Loki. He said that if Loki gets the Eye of Odin, then it will show him that his destiny is to start a war that will destroy all three worlds. All of them, ABE, even ours! Thor thinks that if Loki sees that, if he *knows* it's going to happen no matter what, then he'll start the war now instead of maybe thousands of years in the future."

ABE slumped, his mouth open.

"I know it's scary," Pru said. "And I'll totally understand if you want to go back to the Henhouse. But I think someone has to stop Loki . . . and I think we're the only ones who can."

"But, Mister Fox . . ."

"Can't. He would if he could, but he can't. Long story. But I think that there's a good chance I can sneak in and steal the Eye. We're unnoticeable, remember?" Pru tried to smile, but the thought of what awaited her made it hard.

"Yeah, unnoticeable." ABE ran a hand through his hair. He sighed. "Well, if you're going, I'm going with you. I guess. I can't let you go alone."

"You're sure?" Pru tried not to sound as relieved as she felt.

"I'm sure," ABE said, and his voice barely squeaked at all as he stood up straighter. "If it will stop a war, we have to keep Loki from the Eye."

"Mister Fox was right about you. You do see the truth of things. And I was wrong, ABE, about the stuff I said in the schoolyard the other day. I'm sorry. You're as brave as anyone I know."

"You wouldn't say that if you knew how scared I am right now. Now come on, before we both chicken out."

They moved as quickly as they could without making too much noise. Fortunately, the moss-covered ground softened their steps. Before long, ABE put a hand on Pru's arm and gestured to a break between two roots ahead.

Peering through the crack, Pru saw roughly a dozen giants gathered in a small clearing, a spot where the lattice of roots overhead thinned enough to reveal the sky beyond. The giants all looked up at the great root of Yggdrasil. Pru's eyes were drawn elsewhere. She focused on another person in the clearing, a person she'd spent time with almost every day for the past week but had never seen before in her life.

Loki.

He wore a rich green and brown tunic fit for a king,

and his black hair curled around his face. Oddly, there was something of Fay in his appearance. If Pru hadn't known better, she'd have guessed they were mother and son.

Loki's appearance surprised Pru. She had expected him to look like Thor and Odin in his true form. But they had been all muscles and hair. Loki, with his smooth face and slim build, appeared to be cut from a different cloth. Which, Pru remembered, he was. Loki was a giant and not a god.

Except . . . he didn't look like the giants gathered in the clearing, either. They bore a closer resemblance to Thor and Odin, only the giants were even rougher looking.

And bigger?

Pru wasn't sure about that. Time and distance worked differently in Worlds of Myth. Pru wondered if maybe size did, too. Perhaps beings from Asgard could appear whatever size they wanted. If that was true, Pru wondered why Loki chose to appear the same size as the mortals and gods and not the giants.

"Bah!" one of the giants shouted. "I'm growing tired of this waiting, godling."

ABE stiffened and Pru turned to him and raised a questioning eyebrow.

"That's Gristling," ABE said, swallowing. "He's the

one Mister Fox banished from the fort that day. He's kind of holding a grudge. When Fay, I mean *Loki*, first brought me to him, Gristling kept asking if he could eat me."

"Be patient," Loki said to the giant. "Once I have the Eye of Odin, I'll have the foreknowledge necessary to shape the future to my—our—liking."

"So you say. You say many things. Some of us think you talk too much, godling."

"Have a care, Gristling," Loki hissed. "I told you never to call me that."

Before Gristling could respond, one of the other giants called out, "Look!" and pointed to the sky.

Pru followed the giant's outstretched arm. There, high above, another giant clung to Yggdrasil's side the way a rock climber clings to a steep cliff face.

"At last!" Loki cried.

"Oh no," ABE whispered. "The giant they sent to get the Eye is coming back."

Gristling stepped to the front of the gathering. "What is the fool doing?"

Pru squinted. The giant on Yggdrasil appeared to be swatting at something about his head. He looked like someone trying to drive off an irritating fly.

"Ratatosk!" Pru whispered, feeling a flutter of hope in her chest.

"But what's he doing?" ABE asked.

Pru wondered the same thing. Ratatosk was no match for a giant, though Pru had to admit he seemed to be holding his own. The frost giant's position was precarious. He could only spare one hand to defend himself as Ratatosk danced in and out, running along the giant's back, neck, and shoulders and escaping before the giant could grab him.

Pru understood Ratatosk's intentions a moment later when a pouch that must have been tied around the frost giant's neck broke free. The cord obviously had fallen victim to Ratatosk's teeth.

"No!" Loki's cry cut through the air as the pouch spilled its contents and a small object, glowing with reflected sunlight, bounced down the twining network of roots. Ratatosk chased after it, hurtling at breakneck speed as he tried to catch what could only be the Eye of Odin.

"It's going too fast." Pru struggled to keep her voice low as she clutched at ABE's sleeve. "And it's half his size. He won't be able to stop it!"

Apparently reaching the same conclusion, Ratatosk took a different approach. As the Eye neared the ground, Ratatosk burst into a sprint and, leaping, collided with the bouncing Eye, striking it with his head and changing its direction with all the skill of a World Cup soccer star. The Eye picked up even more speed.

It hit the ground and bounded away from the clustered giants.

"Stop him!" Gristling shouted, as Ratatosk leapt from the tree after the Eye.

Weaving in and out and through the bumbling giants as they tried to follow his progress, Ratatosk used his head, legs, and even his tail to keep the Eye rolling away from the others. He'd soon broken free of the crowd of giants, who couldn't keep track of his wild movements. It seemed the perfect plan, except . . .

"It's slowing," ABE said.

He was right. Ratatosk had bought some time, but now that the Eye was on level ground it was slowing down. Pru felt Ratatosk's panic as each new attempt to control the direction and momentum of the Eye met with less success. He'd managed to get the Eye clear of Loki and the giants momentarily, but they'd soon regroup and catch him.

She had no choice. Pru burst from the tree line and shouted, "Ratatosk, this way!"

So much for unnoticeable.

A shout arose from the giants as they saw her and, for just a moment, her eyes locked with Loki's. Even with everything happening around her, she couldn't help enjoying his shocked expression at her unexpected appearance.

"Shortwit!" Ratatosk said. His relief at seeing her

was clear, despite his choice of greeting, as he leapt up onto Pru's shoulder when she bent to scoop up the Eye. "You made it. It's about time."

"You're welcome," Pru said as she turned back to where she'd left a very startled ABE. Pushing past ABE and plunging into the roots of Yggdrasil, she shouted, "Run!"

CHAPTER
23

PRU WAS GRATEFUL FOR TWO THINGS AS SHE AND ABE ran. First, that Asgard's magical environment allowed her to run just as fast as she could without getting winded. Second, for the first time in her life, she was glad to be a bit small for her age. She'd purposely set off toward a spot where Yggdrasil's roots grew particularly close together. Her small size and ABE's allowed them to dash through the jungle of growth—leaping, ducking, and dodging obstacles as they went. The giants lacked that agility and their brute force only got them so far. Pru heard shouts and curses behind her as the giants tried to tear their way through the dense tangle.

"Follow me!" Pru called to ABE as branches and

roots passed by and between them in a blur. "I can lead us back to the Henhouse."

"Okay. You know, we might actually get away with—"

Before ABE could finish his thought, an enormous hand burst through the branches and grabbed him by the coat, lifting him from the ground.

"ABE!" Pru stopped short, forcing a suddenly unbalanced Ratatosk to jump clear of her shoulder. She started to turn back toward ABE when another hand broke through the tangle of roots and made a blind grab for her. She had no choice but to veer away as the grasping hand drove her farther from ABE and Ratatosk.

Looking back over her shoulder, Pru saw that ABE had managed to wriggle free from his jacket and drop to the ground. With relief, she returned her attention to the path ahead and saw a patch nearby where the roots grew so closely they formed a warren of limbs and branches for her to rabbit her way through. It would force her farther from ABE, but she had no choice.

"ABE!" she shouted. "Try to get back to where we met! The Henhouse is in the opposite direction of the clearing. Just go straight. Ratatosk, go with him!"

Pru had the looking glass. If she had to, she could always use it to backtrack the way she'd come (assuming she escaped the giants). Without Ratatosk, ABE would be lost. She didn't know if ABE heard her, or if he would be able to find the spot where they had met. But it was all she could do as she slipped through a particularly tight space.

Pru scrambled through the bramble of roots and limbs. When she realized that the sounds of pursuit had faded, she settled into a shaded burrow, surrounded by the musty scents of dirt and damp wood. She glanced at her watch, figuring she could stay there until the giants gave up or passed her. Then she would circle back and try to find ABE on her way to the Henhouse.

In the dim light of her hiding place, Pru's eyes were drawn to the strange artifact now in her possession. The Eye of Odin was a small milky-white object about the size of a tennis ball. Pru turned it in her hands, looking for signs of damage from its fall from the heights of Yggdrasil. As she studied the Eye, she became dimly aware that the sounds of pursuit seemed to be growing louder. The Eye captivated her, though. The closer she looked, the more it appeared that there was movement beneath the Eye's surface. No sooner had the thought occurred to her than a darker mass surfaced from the interior of the Eye, a black spot surrounded by an iris of blue flecked with gold.

Only then did Pru remember that, according to the

story, the Eye of Odin was Odin's actual eye. A wave of revulsion swept through Pru, but she couldn't release the Eye. It held her in its gaze. Pru stared into the Eye of Odin, and the Eye of Odin stared back at her.

☆

Pru had remained in one place too long. Distracted by what the Eye had shown her, she didn't hear the sounds of the giants as they closed in on her, step by deadly step. By the time she was aware of them, it was too late.

Gristling ripped apart the roots that were supposed to hide her and grabbed her with one massive hand. Pru kicked and screamed and tried to use her elbows, but it did no good as the giant carried her back to Loki.

When they arrived at the clearing, Gristling tossed Pru to the ground. She landed next to ABE. Ratatosk was there, too.

Pru dropped the Eye of Odin as she hit the ground. It rolled again, only this time it rolled right to Loki's feet. He picked it up with a look of awe and triumph on his face. The frost giants flinched as Loki touched the Eye, clearly afraid of Odin's magic.

Loki, Gristling, and Pru exchanged some few, final words, but they did nothing to change Pru's fate or the fate of her friends. They were surrounded. There was no escape. Gristling closed in for the kill.

Pru screamed.

☆

Pru knelt in the darkness of her hiding place, safe and alone. Sweat poured down her neck.

What had happened?

She glanced at the glowing ball in her hands and then quickly looked away. She'd peered into the Eye of Odin, and the Eye had shown her a vision of the future.

But it had all seemed so real!

Events had unfolded as if she were living them. The only difference was that there had been no sound. She'd only seen the future; she hadn't heard it. (Pru supposed that made sense. After all, it wasn't the Ear of Odin.)

Pru shook her head, trying to erase the memory. A glance at her watch told her the vision had only lasted moments, despite how long it had seemed.

She was breathing heavily. She knew so from the rapid rise and fall of her chest. She couldn't hear herself gasping, because her other senses were slow to awaken after the vision. She had to calm down. Now that she'd seen the future, she told herself, maybe she could change it. She *would* change it.

An unwelcome voice surfaced in Pru's memory.

"All stories are written in stone." Hilde had said so at Winterhaven House.

As her hearing returned to normal, Pru began to be aware of the sound of creaking limbs and breaking wood. Still somewhat dazed, she struggled to understand the threat.

Pru had remained in one place too long. Distracted by what the Eye had shown her, she didn't hear the sounds of the giants as they closed in on her, step by deadly step. By the time she was aware of them, it was too late.

Gristling ripped apart the roots that were supposed to hide her and grabbed her with one massive hand. Pru kicked and screamed and tried to use her elbows, but it did no good as the giant carried her back to Loki.

When they arrived at the clearing, Gristling tossed Pru to the ground. She landed next to ABE. Ratatosk was there, too.

Pru dropped the Eye of Odin as she hit the ground. It rolled again, only this time it rolled right to Loki's feet. He picked it up with a look of awe and triumph on his face. The frost giants flinched as Loki touched the Eye, clearly afraid of Odin's magic.

"Finally," Loki said. "Finally, I hold my own fate in my hands." He tightened his fist around the Eye and turned to Pru. He managed to look sincere. "Prudence Potts. You, young lady, have an extraordinary talent for finding yourself in the middle of things that don't involve you and are certain to land you in a great deal of trouble. On any other day, it's a talent I would applaud. I'm truly sorry you and ABE stumbled into this. I bore you no bad will. I rather liked you both, in fact. You're clever. I don't often get to enjoy the company of clever people."

"Does that mean you'll let us go?" ABE asked.

"No," Loki said, glancing at Gristling. "I'm afraid that's not an option, ABE."

"Enough!" Gristling roared. "You have your prize, godling, now I'll have mine. These two shamed me in battle. I'll be rid of them, and then we'll move on to what must happen next."

Gristling bore down on them, just as he had in Pru's vision.

"I will rend the flesh from your bones. I will clean my teeth with your remains!"

Pru searched desperately for a means of escape, but it was no use. She knew just what would happen next. Loki and Gristling would speak, then she would, and then Gristling would move in for the kill and Pru would scream and that would be the end.

Scream.

She would scream.

"You'd be surprised by how many of life's little problems can be solved by taking either a closer look at the problem—or a closer look at yourself." Those were Mister Fox's words.

She.

Would.

Scream.

"Wait," Loki ordered.

"Why?" Gristling roared his frustration. "I will not be denied."

"No, of course you won't," Loki said. "You're a fierce, grizzled warrior, and you mean a terrible fate for these two children. Is that right?"

"Yes!"

"I thought as much." Loki sounded bored. But curiosity shone in his eyes as they moved from Gristling to Pru. "What I find interesting is that I'm sure these two children must realize your terrible intentions, too. So has it occurred to you, Gristling, to wonder why the girl is smiling?"

Gristling crouched to peer into Pru's face. She had to turn her head away from his cold and fetid breath. Her smile remained firmly in place.

"Perhaps the brat is slow and does not understand her doom," he growled.

"Slow? This one? I don't think so." Stepping between Gristling and Pru, Loki said, in almost a whisper, "Tell me, Pru. I must know. Why *are* you smiling?"

"Well," Pru said, "I guess you could say I'm smiling for three reasons." ABE and Ratatosk were looking at her with nearly as much curiosity as Loki. When Loki arched an eyebrow, Pru explained.

"First, I'm smiling because the sun came out this morning, just before I left for Asgard. That's always nice. I like the sun."

Gristling scoffed, but Loki frowned, slightly.

"Second, I'm smiling because I'm on a whole new world. I mean, we're not on Midgard anymore. And, you know, travel can be so exciting."

Loki's frown deepened.

"And the third reason I'm smiling," Pru said, raising her eyes to meet Loki's, "is because I know how to do something only the best detectives can do. I know how to read lips—including my own."

A look of understanding blossomed on Loki's face, a moment too late, unfortunately for him. Even as Loki drew his breath to speak, Pru's hand slipped into her messenger bag. It slid past her father's badge. The shield couldn't help her now. There was no place left to hide. And she was done hiding, anyway. Instead, her fist tightened around another item in the bag.

Pru screamed, "*Thor!*"

CHAPTER
24

SILENCE DEVOURED THE CLEARING.

A moment passed.

Another.

"Pathetic." Gristling began to laugh, though there was a nervous edge to his laughter that no one missed. "You wasted your last breath in a useless call for help. You shame your fathers and starve ravens with your cowardice!"

Pru withdrew her hand from her messenger bag and dangled the object she held in front of her. It was the amulet Thor had given her.

"No!" Gristling hissed as dark clouds formed in the sky above.

"Just so you know," Pru said, with a glance at ABE,

"I don't think of it as being a coward. I think of it as using good judgment to plan for the future."

"Prudence," said an awed ABE, who was an excellent person to have around when defining a word, or redefining oneself.

"Oh, and Loki?" Pru called out.

Loki tore his panicked gaze away from the dark clouds above to look at Pru.

"Just so you know? You may be the Lord of Lies, but I'm the better Fibber."

Loki stared at Pru as a low rumble began to fill the air. To Pru's great surprise, he mouthed the words "Very clever, indeed," just before a thunderclap tore through the clearing and knocked everyone, including the giants, from their feet. The Eye of Odin tumbled from Loki's hand as a voice boomed through the clearing.

"Loki, what strange company you're keeping."

When Pru recovered from the blast of sound, Thor stood in the center of the clearing, an inferno of fiery hair and temper. He looked just like Pru remembered him, except now he held a vicious-looking war hammer in a clenched fist.

"Is that really Thor?" ABE whispered as he and Pru regained their footing.

"Yup."

"Wow."

"Totally."

Pru thought she saw the thunder god wink in their direction.

"Thor," Loki said, spreading his arms open in a plea for understanding, "this is not what it looks like. These children were in danger. I pretended to ally myself with the giants so that—"

"Liar!" Gristling roared, climbing back to his feet. The clearing exploded with the rage of the betrayed giants. Thunder boomed as Thor threw himself into battle. He hurled his hammer at his nearest foe, sending the giant toppling into one of his comrades. Wind ripped through the clearing, stirring a blinding cloud of dirt as thunder pounded all around.

"Follow me!" Ratatosk called as he took off through the developing skirmish.

"Wait!" ABE said, and he disappeared for a moment into the cloud of battle.

"ABE, stop! Where are you going?" In a panic, Pru looked from where ABE had vanished in a swirl of dust and flailing giants' limbs to where Ratatosk stood, gesturing her to follow.

Just as she was about to chase after ABE, he reemerged from around the side of a vanquished giant's head. He carried something clutched close to his chest— the Eye of Odin!

"Are you insane?" Pru asked.

"They were going to rend our flesh," ABE protested. "I couldn't just let them keep it."

Pru couldn't argue with that.

"Hurry!" Ratatosk urged.

Somehow, Ratatosk found a safe path through the chaos. How they avoided getting crushed by a falling giant or shattered limb from Yggdrasil, Pru would never know. Ahead, the largest root Pru had seen yet rose up from the ground. An enormous crack split the root in two. Ratatosk led them into the crack and through to the cavernous space that lay beyond.

"We're inside Yggdrasil!" Pru's voice echoed around them.

"So what do we do now? How do we get out of here?" ABE asked.

"Yggdrasil goes everywhere, if you know your way around," Ratatosk explained. "And I know my way better than anyone."

"You mean you can get us home?" Pru asked.

Ratatosk twitched his tail in answer and sped ahead.

Pru and ABE followed. But with her next step, Pru felt only air where the ground had just been solid. She fell to her bottom and began to slide downward through a great, winding, hollow tube. A trickle of water accompanied her on her descent.

"This is just like a water slide!" Pru exclaimed as a sudden weight on her shoulder announced Ratatosk's arrival.

"Fun, yes?" Ratatosk seemed pleased. Pru suspected he hadn't had much opportunity to share his knowledge of Yggdrasil with others. "Water gathers in the roots and feeds the three magic springs!" Ratatosk yelled as the wind roared around them. "This is the fastest way to travel, and the most exhilarating!"

"Just so long as I don't get splinters!" ABE called from just behind them.

The surface beneath was smooth, no doubt from countless eons of flowing water. The ride had so many twists and turns, though, it made the fiercest roller coaster seem like a merry-go-round at a kiddie park.

Eventually, the slope leveled out and Pru and ABE regained their footing. Ratatosk leapt off Pru's shoulder and dashed ahead toward a crack of light. The squirrel slipped through the opening easily, but Pru and ABE had to squeeze their way through. Finally, they emerged, gasping and wet, into the light and the world beyond.

"Where are we?" Pru asked, her eyes still adjusting.

"We're back. Pru, we're back in the cemetery!"

Blinking, Pru took in her surroundings. ABE was right. They stood beneath the shade of an old ash tree in the cemetery, having just emerged from a hole between the tree's gnarled roots.

"We're back! We did it! I can't—"

Wooden shrapnel raked Pru's skin as the ash tree suddenly shattered in an explosion of dirt and wood and Gristling erupted from the tunnel below. A great bruise swelled one of the giant's eyes shut and bloodstains marred his animal-skin tunic.

"You!" he growled. His voice was rock grinding against rock, like the sharpening of a primitive axe, or the placement of stones in a new wall. "You did this. You brought the serpent slayer and destroyed my clan."

Pru staggered back, shocked. Her messenger bag bounced against her, and Pru felt the weight of the fox-head looking glass rebound against her thigh. Her hand dove into the bag, tightening on the wooden handle. If she could just show Gristling his reflection in it, he'd be banished back to Asgard. Pru tensed, waiting for her moment.

"The things I will do to you will be remembered and retold to frighten generations of mortal children to come," Gristling raved. "I will grind you to dust. You will beg for mercy with your last, gurgling breath. I will—"

"Uh . . . sorry," ABE said, politely interrupting the murderous frost giant's rant as a shadow fell over them all. ABE pointed above them. "But is that a giant chicken foot in the sky?"

It was perhaps the oddest thing Pru had ever heard a person say.

The strangest part was, ABE was right.

The unmistakable shape of the Henhouse descended from the skies above. Sticking out from beneath the house, just as unmistakably, was an enormous chicken foot.

Pru watched as it plummeted to Earth and landed—directly on Gristling's head.

✧

"So," Mister Fox said, after he emerged and examined the empty ground beneath the Henhouse. "For the record, it appears you can banish a Mythic back to where it belongs by using an enchanted looking glass or by dropping a house on its head and knocking it unconscious. Good to know," he deadpanned, nodding to himself.

"That was a chicken's foot," Pru pointed out, still stunned. "You have a giant chicken foot stuck to the bottom of your house." It was the sort of thing she thought needed repeating.

"Mind the toes," ABE said, smacking his palm to his forehead.

Pru stared at him, wondering if everyone had decided to go insane and not tell her. "What are you talking about?"

"It's what Mister Fox said when we went into the

Henhouse. Remember? He wasn't talking about our toes."

"No, I wasn't. Baba Yaga had some truly strange ideas about home décor. So, yes, the Henhouse travels by chicken foot. It's surprisingly fuel efficient," Mister Fox said, looking from ABE to Pru, pride evident on his face. "It appears that you were successful, Pru, at bringing back our wayward friend."

"You don't even know the half of it. Show him, ABE," Pru said, too distracted by their recent triumph to dwell on the chicken foot.

ABE held out his hand and Mister Fox reached out to accept the Eye of Odin, a look of wonder on his face.

Mister Fox stared into the Eye of Odin, and it looked to Pru as though the Eye of Odin stared back at him.

A long moment passed before Mister Fox gave his head a small shake. He slipped the Eye into one of his coat pockets as he turned his attention back to Pru and ABE. "I'll have to give some thought as to what to do about that. Now, though, as for you two, I don't say this often, but I might be just a little impressed."

"We three," Pru corrected. "We couldn't have done it without Ratatosk. He was amazing!"

Ratatosk looked up at the praise, and for once was rendered speechless.

It didn't last.

"Well, someone had to look after you two . . ." He paused, and Pru braced herself for the insults sure to follow. "Actually, I suppose you two didn't perform so awfully after all. Quite satisfactory. Adequate even."

"High praise indeed," Mister Fox said, one eyebrow raised. "Still, as touching as this is, Pru and ABE, you two need to get back to your families."

"What?" The sudden dismissal startled Pru. She wasn't done basking in their victory. But then she remembered the circumstances around her leaving that morning. "My mom! Oh no. How long have I been gone? And ABE, he's been gone since yesterday. Our parents must be freaking out!"

"As a matter of fact, they haven't missed you a bit," Mister Fox said. He went on before Pru could object. "Remember, most people's minds are closed to magic. So whenever someone from this world travels to a World of Myth, that person slips from the minds of people who know him or her. Your families missed you while you were gone, yes, but they didn't know what they were missing. Now that you're back, they'll be anxious for you. You need to go to them and reassure them. They'll be a little confused, but all they'll really care about is that you're home. So go. But come back tomorrow to tell me about what happened. I have a thing or two to take care of."

"You'll still be here tomorrow?" Pru asked.

"I'll be here."

"You promise?"

"Would I lie?"

Pru found her house empty when she arrived. After quickly putting on dry clothes, she made her way to the Explorers' Fair. Despite what Mister Fox had said, Pru expected a scolding for sneaking out that morning. Instead, her mother just seemed very happy to see Pru as she ran up.

Pru was a little surprised at just how happy she felt seeing her mother, too. It felt like they'd been apart a very long time. They embraced with equal enthusiasm. When their hug ended, and it did not end soon, Pru's mother cupped her daughter's chin in her hand.

"Listen, sweetie . . . I've been thinking about what you said last night."

"I know, Mom. I'm sorry. I was just really upset about something and—"

"No, listen." Pru's mother took a deep breath and looked Pru in the eye. "You're right. I haven't been able to make this world as safe a place for you as I'd like it to be. And I'm sorry for that, honey. I'm so sorry. But you have to understand something. I'm your mother, Pru. That means one thing. I'm always going to try. Whether you like it or not, I'm always going to try."

It was the first honest moment Pru felt like she'd

had with her mother in a long, long time. She wanted it to go on forever.

So, naturally, that's when Mrs. Edleman appeared.

"Mrs. Potts. Prudence. How nice to see you," Mrs. Edleman said with about as much enthusiasm as Pru felt at seeing her teacher on a Saturday. "I hope you're enjoying your day."

"We're certainly glad for the change in the weather. Isn't that right, Pru?"

"I suppose." Only then did Pru realize that the clouds had vanished completely from the skies above.

"Yes, well, that's something we can all agree on," Mrs. Edleman said. "Though I'm surprised, Mrs. Potts, that you allowed Prudence the opportunity to come out today. I know you were quite worried when you called the school yesterday after Prudence didn't go straight home."

Pru's mother frowned at the reminder. "Yes, I was upset. And there will be consequences. But the Explorers' Fair is once a year. I'm sure you understand."

"Of course," Mrs. Edleman said, sounding not at all like she meant it. "Well, I expect you'll be glad to hear that I had a word or two with Prudence about how important it is for her to stop these ridiculous investigations of hers. I'm certain that if we both remind her that she is an eleven-year-old child and not, in fact, a detective, then these worrisome incidents will come to an end."

"Excuse me?" Pru's mother said in a tone that startled Pru. "Mrs. Edleman, you have no idea how grateful I am to you for the . . . patience you've shown with Pru this year. Her behavior over the whole 'Schoolyard Sasquatch' incident was inexcusable, and I promise you she is still facing consequences at home from *that* little stunt." Pru cringed at the look she got from her mother.

"But," Pru's mother continued, "with all due respect, Mrs. Edleman, if my daughter chooses to think of herself as a detective, then I'm proud of that choice. Everett would be, too. Though she may still have to learn that detectives use their talents to stop trouble, not start it, I happen to think Pru has the makings of a fine detective.

"And if you think that an eleven-year-old can't be a detective, then you either don't quite understand what it is that detectives do, or you don't remember being eleven years old yourself. I do hope you enjoy the rest of this beautiful day, Mrs. Edleman."

Pru followed in her mother's wake as she walked away, gazing up at her in awe. "Mom, you just totally told Mrs. Edleman off!"

"Don't be silly, Pru. I did nothing of the sort. I had

an adult discussion with your teacher, that's all. And she *is* your teacher, Pru. She sets the rules while you're at school. Luckily for you," Pru's mother added with a wink, "you're not at school today."

It had been a long time since Pru had held her mother's hand, and it felt strange somehow as they set off to enjoy the fair together. Pru wasn't sure if her mother's hand felt smaller or if it was her own hand that felt bigger, not quite as small for her age.

CHAPTER 25

PRU ARRIVED IN THE CEMETERY WITH ABE ON SUN-day morning to find Mister Fox and Ratatosk sitting on the porch of the Henhouse. They were talking in low voices but stopped when Pru and ABE approached.

"All hail the conquering heroes," Mister Fox said with a tip of his hat. "You're just in time to hear the news."

"What news?" Pru asked.

"Yesterday, after you left, our furry friend here filled me in on some of the details of your adventure. After hearing some of what you all went through, I asked Ratatosk to return to Asgard and do a little scouting. He was just giving me a report."

"And?" ABE asked.

"Thor was resplendently victorious against the giants, yes, yes. But . . . that heath-fire idiot Loki escaped in the confusion," Ratatosk said.

Pru and ABE exchanged nervous glances.

"I can't say I'm surprised," Mister Fox commented. "Loki has a talent for getting himself out of trouble. In fact, he escapes trouble with nearly as much ease as he enters into it."

"But won't he come back?" ABE asked. "To get revenge, or to get the Eye of Odin?"

"I don't think so," Mister Fox said. "I think you two are safe from him and Gristling for the time being. Thor caused some serious damage, and Loki's scheming created some friction between him and the giants. He'll smooth things over. That's what he does. It will take time, though. And we're spreading the word that the Eye of Odin is gone, so they won't come looking for that."

"Gone?" Pru and ABE said at the same time.

"Hidden."

"Where?" Pru pressed. "Why?"

"Because a little knowledge of the future might be helpful on the rare occasion, but you can have too much of a good thing. Odin learned that the hard way. I don't want anyone else to suffer the same fate." Mister Fox looked at Pru as he spoke.

"But it saved our lives! I wanted a chance to look in it again."

"Why? To see all the secrets of the future laid bare? To always know what will happen, and when? To feel safe and certain?" Mister Fox peered at Pru. "Is that really what you want?"

Pru sighed. "No. I guess not. Not *completely*, anyway. But it would be nice to know when Mrs. Edleman planned to spring a pop quiz on us."

"I suppose I failed to consider the vital role an artifact of such awesome power might have on your ability to pass a pop quiz," Mister Fox said. "Shame on me. Ah, well, opportunities lost. But on to other things, though they pale in comparison. Ratatosk gave me the bare bones of yesterday's story, but I still want to hear the details from the two of you."

They sat on the porch of the Henhouse and took turns retelling everything that had taken place over the past couple of days. Everyone had something to say, especially Ratatosk, who did not often get to speak so many of his own words. And, naturally, everyone had questions. Facing Pru, Mister Fox went first.

"All right, I've gone over it again and again and I have to ask. How did you get inside the Henhouse?"

"Oh, that." Pru cleared her throat. "Um, it's possible I read your lips, that day outside the Henhouse.

I saw you whisper something, and when I repeated it, the door to the Henhouse appeared."

"Reading lips? That's a difficult thing to do. It's also incredibly sneaky. I'm impressed."

"You're not mad?"

"Mad?" Mister Fox leaned back, resting his weight on his elbows. "For sneaking into the Henhouse? Hardly. How do you think I first got into Baba Yaga's house?"

"I have a question," ABE said, also turning to Pru. "How did you know Thor would answer your call?"

"I wondered that, too," Mister Fox said.

Pru pulled Thor's amulet from her bag and showed it to Mister Fox and ABE.

"Thor gave this to me when I found him in the jail. He said people used it when they called on him for help, a long time ago. I kind of forgot about it for a while because Thor made it clear he wasn't going to disobey his dad by leaving the jail or interfering on Midgard. But when I thought about the vision I saw in the Eye of Odin, I realized that the last thing I screamed was actually Thor's name."

"You read your own lips in your vision of the future?" Mister Fox asked. "Brilliant!"

Pru blushed. "I didn't understand at first. Why would I scream for Thor when he was locked up and refused to help? Then I remembered. The sun came out yesterday when Mister Fox and I were in the cemetery, just before I left for Asgard. I figured all those clouds we'd had were because Thor was locked in our jail and the weather reflected his mood. The sun must have broken through because Thor wasn't in jail anymore."

"I'm sure Odin released him as soon as Loki left for Asgard," Mister Fox said, nodding.

"And we weren't on Midgard anymore, either," Pru added. "Odin only said Thor couldn't interfere with events on Midgard. Since I was in Asgard, I figured calling for help was fair game."

"You were amazing," ABE said. "All I did was get captured."

"No way," Pru objected. "You figured out who Fay was even before I did. And you ran through a battle-field to get the Eye of Odin. That was one of the bravest things I ever saw."

ABE ran a hand through his hair, but he also smiled.

Pru shifted in her seat and focused on Mister Fox. "Now it's my turn to ask a question: If you knew Loki was involved like you said, how come you didn't use your looking glass to find Loki in the town? If I used it to track down ABE on Asgard, how come you couldn't use it to track down Loki here?"

"I tried. There was too much interference. Thor's tantrum charged the whole atmosphere around Middleton with magical energy. The closer I got to town, the worse it was. Every once in a while I'd catch a hint of a trail. That's why I was in town that day when you two saw me. But the trail kept dissolving. It wasn't until Loki stood directly in front of me in the cemetery that night that I was able to identify him with the looking glass."

"How come you didn't tell me it was him?" Pru asked, thinking of all the trouble it would have saved them.

"Because at that time, I didn't even know if you knew who Loki was. Besides, would you have believed me?"

"No," Pru admitted, remembering how frightened she'd been of Mister Fox at the time.

"Hold on a second," ABE said. "You knew we saw you that day we followed you to the fort?"

"I'd be a pretty poor detective if I didn't know when someone was watching me."

"How come you didn't say anything?" Pru asked.

"I was curious. I wanted to see what you'd do. Though I might have handled things differently if I'd known what waited at the fort. You weren't prepared for that. Still, everything worked out."

"There's something else," ABE said. "That day we followed you we noticed that the people around you acted weird."

"That's right! They acted like they couldn't see

you, like you were unnoticeable. Like a Mythic." Pru peered at Mister Fox, a hint of suspicion clouding the otherwise perfect day.

"Very good," Mister Fox said, reclining further and stretching his legs. "You're right. But I'm not a Mythic, Pru, so you can stop looking at me like that. I was born here just like you and ABE. But remember, I did spend half my life traveling Worlds of Myth in the Henhouse. So while I don't belong there in those worlds, I don't belong here in this one anymore, either. Not completely. I'm able to pass unnoticed here, just as you were able to pass unnoticed in Asgard."

"That explains why people didn't really see you," ABE said. "But I've also been wondering how come people *could* see Fay. She was a Mythic, after all."

"But she didn't appear as one," Mister Fox explained. "People wouldn't have seen Loki, but Fay fit the idea of something people expected to see. That's why people in town could see Old Man Grimnir, too. He didn't appear as Odin. You see, even people who can't see Mythics are aware of their presence on a basic level. They're the movements out of the corner of the eye. The shifting shadows of the shouldn't-be. So when a Mythic is around, the minds of people who can't see Mythics create reasonable explanations for them."

"So Fay and Old Man Grimnir were reasonable explanations," ABE said, nodding.

"Does that mean that if the giants *had* attacked, people's minds would have created reasonable explanations for the damage they did?" Pru asked.

"Exactly. Those giants would have destroyed Middleton. But survivors would have reported a tornado had swept through the town, or something like that. Oftentimes, when the news reports natural disasters as 'acts of God,' they're right, more or less. They just don't know which god. Now, before I forget, there's something I want to give you two."

The detective rose and went inside. When he returned, he carried two miniature Henhouses. Each was the size of a dollhouse, though crafted with such detail that Pru could see the porch, the round window, and the weather vane at the very top. In fact, the only difference that Pru could see (besides size) between the miniature Henhouses and the real one was that the Henhouses Mister Fox carried each had a handle extending up from the roof. As Mister Fox set the miniatures down beside her and ABE, Pru noticed that one of the boxes was just a bit larger than the other.

"Consider these tokens of appreciation, or maybe tools of the trade," Mister Fox said. "The front panel opens. Look inside."

Pru pulled on the doorknob and the front face of her Henhouse swung open. Inside was a looking glass just like Mister Fox's except for the sculpted squirrel's head that adorned the bottom of Pru's glass's handle in place of the fox head on the original.

"It seemed appropriate," Mister Fox said, looking over her shoulder. "Only the rarest of creatures can travel between the worlds these days."

Ratatosk had lost interest in the conversation when it moved away from his role and decided to stretch out and enjoy the sun. Now, he roused himself and settled on one of Pru's shoulders to admire his likeness on Pru's glass. "Dashing. Very, very handsome."

"And for you, ABE, the raven seemed right for someone who sees so much," Mister Fox said.

Pru looked over to see that ABE held a glass like hers but with a raven at the base of its handle.

"Cool!" Pru tested the weight of hers in her hand. "Are they magic?"

"They're enchanted, yes, much like mine."

"Thanks," ABE said. "It's . . . amazing." He shifted in his seat, his eyes locked on the looking glass he held in his lap.

"Is something wrong, ABE? Not a fan of ravens?" Mister Fox asked.

"No, it's not that. It's just . . . I feel bad. After Pru talked to Thor, she asked me what I thought of you. And, at the time, I wasn't sure. I was really scared of everything that was happening, actually. And I was a little scared of you. Pru knew better. I think I just confused her more and made it easier for Loki to trick her."

"No, ABE," Pru said before Mister Fox could speak. "You were just being honest. It's sort of your thing. And besides, you weren't wrong." She met the detective's eyes. "Mister Fox isn't dangerous, but being around him's not exactly safe, either, if you think about the work he does."

Mister Fox tipped his hat in acknowledgment of the fact.

"Pru's quite right, ABE. There's nothing to apologize for."

"But while we're talking about you, I have one more question," Pru said, studying the detective. "Why do you live in the cemetery? It's kind of gloomy, isn't it?"

"It's not really my choice. Witches are magical creatures. They build their houses to exist on the borderlands between this world and Worlds of Myth. The Henhouse is no exception. For some reason, though, when I moved in, the Henhouse began only to set foot—forgive the pun—on lands that were also on the border between the living and the dead, graveyards and such. It might be because I'm mortal, and not a witch. Or maybe the Henhouse has a morbid sense of humor."

Almost as if the Henhouse knew it was the subject of discussion, a creaking sound reached Pru's ears and she looked up to see the weather vane atop the Henhouse begin to shift.

"Ah," Mister Fox said, rising, "duty calls."

"What do you mean?" Pru asked.

"The Henhouse has a whiff of trouble brewing somewhere."

"Another Mythic crossing into our world?" ABE asked, rising and stepping down from the porch.

"Looks that way." Mister Fox's voice carried an edge of excitement.

"So you're leaving? Already?" Pru asked, dislodging Ratatosk as she jumped off the steps and landed next to ABE. Ratatosk scampered up to perch on Mister Fox's shoulder, apparently deciding to try a new method of travel.

The Henhouse began to shift and rose up on its one chicken foot. The detective still stood atop the steps. With one hand, he gripped the railing while, with the other, he held his hat firmly upon his head, high above them.

"It would appear so. Pru and ABE, it was a pleasure meeting you both," Mister Fox called down.

Pru had one question left. She was almost too afraid to ask it, but she was more afraid of not knowing the answer.

"Will we ever see you again?" she called up to Mister Fox.

He appeared to think about it.

"It seems unlikely, doesn't it?" he said. "The mystery is solved, the villain is defeated, and the day is saved. I don't see why our paths would cross again."

The Henhouse crouched, preparing to launch. As it did, it lowered Mister Fox down almost to the level of the ground. He leaned forward and added, with a wink, "And that's the truth."

With that, the Henhouse's single leg straightened and shot the headquarters of The Unbelievable FIB high into the air at a dizzying speed. It vanished quickly, though the detective's whoop of delight lingered in the air a little longer.

"That is the strangest thing I've ever seen," ABE said. "And that's saying something these days." He looked over at Pru, perhaps expecting that she'd need comforting. Instead, he found her looking up into the sky and smiling.

"Are you okay?" he asked.

"I'm great. Why do you ask?"

"Um . . . I guess I thought you'd be sad that he left."

"I am."

"Oh." ABE took a deep breath. "Okay, I'm almost afraid to ask, because the last time someone asked you this question things got pretty insane. But . . . why are you smiling, exactly?"

"Because Mister Fox said it was true that we'd never see him again."

"Right." ABE appeared thoughtful. "No, sorry. I still don't get it."

"He said it was true," Pru repeated, turning her smile on her friend. "But he never said it was *entirely* true."

ACKNOWLEDGMENTS

I'm extremely grateful to the many people who helped this story complete its journey to publication. It's a journey that began with Ammi-Joan Paquette, my agent, and ended with Elise Howard, my editor. Both Joan and Elise were everything a new author could hope for in an agent and editor—they were honest, supportive, knowledgeable, and (most of all) very patient.

There were also many people who helped along the way. I'm grateful to the many folks at Algonquin Young Readers who helped in the book's development in so many ways, including Hannah Allaman, Sarah Alpert, Kelly Bowen, Emma Boyer, Robin Cruise, Brooke Csuka, Brunson Hoole, Eileen Lawrence, Debra Linn, Krestyna Lypen, Lauren Moseley, Craig Popelars, Chad Royal, and Ina Stern.

I'm also grateful to my readers, including Nancy Ruth Patterson, Stacey Donahoe, Frances Kelley Prescott, Joan Domin, Karen Lindeborg, Elaine Vickers, and Jane LeGrow—who went above and beyond in her support by agreeing to marry me over the course of this journey, which was very generous of her, I think, and for which I am particularly grateful.

Finally, tracing the story's development back to its very beginning, I learned a lot about what kinds of stories I enjoy sharing with children through the work I've done with them. I am grateful to everyone who has given me the opportunities I've had to do that work, including Rebecca McNulty, David Taylor, Richard Virgin, Sally Myers, Adriana DeGrafft, and Laureen Pierandi. And, of course, I am grateful to all the young people who have taught me so much over the years.